VOTAN

Well, if you really want t[...]
chained to an oak tree, half [...]
with wolves trying to eat m[...]
it's not nearly as interestin[...]

I married two queens, and seduced one, and that taught me to be very wary about Barbarian women. I reorganised a trading firm, and I sent half Germany money-mad. I made one king and I killed another; I led an army into battle, and won, and I made up at least four hundred songs about it that you may hear in any barracks in the Empire where there are German auxiliary cavalry.

It isn't every man you meet who can remember being worshipped as a God – and who still is. And it isn't every day you meet someone who has fathered half a dozen Royal Houses. I was young, then . . .

VOTAN

John James

BANTAM BOOKS
TORONTO · NEW YORK · LONDON · SYDNEY · AUCKLAND

VOTAN

A BANTAM BOOK   0 553 17358 8

Originally published in Great Britain by Cassell & Co. Ltd.

PRINTING HISTORY

Cassell & Co. edition published 1966
Universal-Tandem Publishing Co. edition published 1971
Bantam edition published 1987

This book is set in 10/11pt Plantin.

Bantam Books are published by Transworld Publishers Ltd.,
61-63 Uxbridge Road, Ealing, London W5 5SA, in Australia by
Transworld Publishers (Australia) Pty. Ltd., 15-23 Helles
Avenue, Moorebank, NSW 2170, and in New Zealand by Transworld
Publishers (N.Z.) Ltd., Cnr. Moselle and Waipareira Avenues,
Henderson, Auckland.

Printed and bound in Great Britain by
Cox & Wyman Ltd., Reading, Berks.

Vindabonum

1

Well, if you really want to know how it was I came to be chained to an oak tree, half-way up in the middle of nowhere, with wolves trying to eat me out of it, I'll tell you. Of course, it's not nearly as interesting as what happened afterwards, but you can piece that together yourself if you go down to any of the taverns around the Praetorian barracks and listen to what the soldiers sing. If you can understand German, of course. They sing things like:

> High the Allfather
> Hung in the hornbeam;
> Nine days and no drinking,
> Nine nights and no nurture . . .

or:

> Alfege the Earl, Odin-born,
> Great in guile, wise in war . . .

I often go down there and listen. It never crosses their minds that it was only me all the time. Half the songs are about me; the other half I made up myself, anyway.

I thought that would make you sit up. It isn't every man you meet who can remember being worshipped as a God — and who still is. And it isn't every day you meet someone who has fathered half a dozen Royal Houses. I haven't spent all my time in the counting house, you know. As a matter of fact, looking back, I seem to have spent most of it in bed. That's where I learnt my German, in bed, with Ursa, in Vindabonum.

5

I was young, then. We went up to Vindabonum, my father and I, during the reign of his late Sainted Majesty. It was not altogether by our own volition. We were priests of Apollo in the Old City. Not Apollo the Sun only, or Apollo the Music-maker at all, but Apollo the Healer, who is a very specialised God indeed and not to be found in very many shrines. There was a great deal to do there in those days. People came to be healed from quite a distance, sprains and bruises and such like, mostly. My father was very good with these.

'Yes, yes, Photinus,' he would say, 'it's all very well to do these spectacular cures, trepannings and amputations and visitations of boils and sores. But how often do you get a chance to see them? Not often enough to get any practice in, let alone make any money. No, it's these little jobs that are the doctor's bread and oil. They come in every day by the score. They've got to come in, you see. You can follow the plough with boils or even if you're raving mad – you can govern a province like that, you know – but not with a swollen ankle that you can't put to the ground. You've got your choice: come in to the doctor and pay, or lie up for a fortnight, and you can't afford to do that. In you have to go, half a day in the ox cart, see the doctor, pay up your half piece of silver or your pair of chickens, and zut! he jerks it back into place for you. The next day, back you are behind the plough or pitching sheaves into the wagon, and you know that the next winter you won't starve. Time's everything in sowing and harvest; do it when you have to or never do it at all.'

Not that we were too worried about the pairs of chickens. Some of the hill farms had been in the family since the Persians, and a lot of the other charters weren't much later. And there was some confusion, very often, about what was Temple property and what was family. So long as we lived in Vindabonum, the silver came up regularly. From the farm rents, from the olive presses, from the shipping line, from all the agencies we had. Not a bad organisation really. It all came through keeping out of politics.

But it was politics sent us up to Vindabonum. Keeping

6

out of politics is always a bit of a risk. It isn't so much supporting the wrong man as not supporting the right one, and there had been a bit of trouble about not joining up with the right people.

Now doubtless in the days of their late Sainted Majesties Nero or Galba we might have all been killed where we sat, but by my young days we'd run out of violence. Besides we had a lot of influence in odd places, and it was enough for someone to suggest, quite firmly, that it might be better if we went and lived elsewhere for a time. Not necessarily Vindabonum. They offered us a choice of several places, all quite horrible, like that place south of Leptis Magna, on the edge of the desert, and York. I never did get to York.

Anyway, they were all on frontiers, and we happened to have an agent in Vindabonum, a man called Otho who did a lot of buying of furs and timber and wax across the Danube, and selling cloth and wine and pottery and oil. That's a good trade; you sell the oil and wine *in* the pots, saves carriage. So we went there, up with all our furniture and plate in the wagons from Aquileia, we weren't going to be uncomfortable, and our own servants. We had a dreadful time with them, and in the end we had to send them back and stock up in the local slave market.

That's how we got Ursa. She was a Thuringian who had been carried off by a party of scavenging Marcomen, a big hearty lass, blonde and blue eyed. Don't you believe it when they tell you all Germans have yellow hair. A lot of them have, enough to impress you, but most of them are more mousy. As for red hair, that Tacitus talks about, that's rare too, except among the Picts. Fair skin, though, mostly, and nobody quite as black-haired or black-eyed as we see here in the south.

When we got Ursa, she was none too worried about what had happened. Being hauled off to Vindabonum and sold for rough work in the kitchen was, for her, an entry into the great world. She didn't stay in the kitchen long. I was nineteen at the time, and very much at a loss, and there wasn't anything much she could do about it, even if she had objected. In fact, she seemed really pleased at my picking her up, and somehow the other Germans in the household always treated her as something special. And that's how I learned German.

Once I began to get fluent in German, Vindabonum, too, began to wake up. Hardly any of the locals spoke Greek. A lot of them could be understood in a rather horrid kind of Latin, but mostly it was German or nothing. Once I could get along in German it was different. It was another world, their world. It was a world of small shops and taverns, open markets and bustling people. Savages at bottom, of course, like their cousins across the Danube, noisy and uncontrollable.

I was nineteen, I told you, and there wasn't much of what you might call entertainment. There was a kind of theatre where they had regimental sports twice a year, second-rate gladiators and beasts nobody would risk on a more sophisticated audience. There was a tale locally about a party of actors who had come with some Sophocles, but nobody turned up, and they were last seen walking back to Aquileia, having sold all their costumes to pay their debts, and lucky nobody sold them too.

So the only things to watch were the religious ceremonies, not that there were very many of them either. There were the usual official shrines and the troops had a Mithraeum, but that was private, of course. No use trying to see that unless you're willing to take on more obligations than anyone would in their right minds. I wonder how long it takes to get the bull's blood out of your hair. The Jews were just as private; there were two kinds, the orthodox ones, and the ones who eat anything and worship an ass's head.

There was more fun where the Germans lived, outside the walls, in nasty little slums along the river and the roads. They weren't anything like as bad as the German villages I've seen since, but they shocked me then. They were alive, though, with their little clusters of square thatched houses, and their cooking fires outside and naked children in the dust. If it rained, of course, it was a different matter, and when it snowed it turned quite nasty, especially inside with

8

everyone huddled around the open fires, or braziers if your house doubled as a tavern. But most of the summer and autumn we could sit on the benches outside those taverns, drinking the local brews of barley or rye or plum, and looking at the way these people lived, not lived, camped really, not living in any settled way, squatting under the ramparts.

What did they live on? Well some of them had bits of land out on the edge of the woods, and a lot lived by heavy labour, hauling barges up the Danube or building in the barracks. A lot of them were craftsmen, heavy workers like smiths or potters. It's always a sign of civilisation when you find men doing the potting. The men who worked the wagons up from Aquileia, with all that lovely red Samian, couldn't afford to buy it and they used the local rather gritty ware.

Most of these people had relations across the river on the Marcfield, as they called it, or even farther north. On feast days we would go to one of the riverside taverns, Rudi's usually, and watch them coming across on the ferry. There were peasants in their best clothes come to see the great city, and a very great city that filthy Vindabonum must have seemed to them. They only saw the native quarter, of course; we never let them within the gates.

There were mothers and fathers up to see their recruit sons in the cavalry barracks, because by that time nobody was very choosy who you recruited for an auxiliary regiment, and they brought in pies and sausages. Sweethearts too, sometimes, but not many of those, because half of the recruits were running from some girl they'd got into trouble, and the other half were eager to see if it felt any different to get a southern girl into the same state.

There were pedlars with leather and carved wood, and cheap silver ornaments beaten out of silver coins, and men with Amber, and there were Holy Men. We usually had a line of legionaries across the quay, picking out at random perhaps one traveller in five or six and making him turn out his bundle for concealed weapons. The people didn't seem to mind this, and we never saw anybody caught with anything, although often enough the odd pie or apple

9

changed hands. It made the job worth while, and was one of the reasons why duty on the river was popular even after ten years of peace. But nobody ever filched a piece of Amber, it wouldn't have been worth it, too much scandal. And nobody ever searched a Holy Man.

You've probably read about the Germans' religion in authors like Tacitus. But none of these men ever went across the frontier. None of them ever spoke to more than one or two Germans, and those were Latin-speaking civilised ones, and being properly brought up and full of Homer, they tried to make some sense out of what they heard. The fact of the matter is that there's no sense in it at all. No two Germans will agree on who their Gods are. Mostly they have two. One is called Tiwaz, and he is a fine-weather Wind God, and the other is called Wude, and he is a bad-weather Sky God, and you hear him riding overhead with all his dogs howling in any storm. In the north, they also have a kind of Vulcan, a Smith God, who must be very comforting in the winters they have there. And there are a lot of minor Gods for streams and trees and suchlike, but nobody agrees about them at all.

They haven't any real temples; they make offerings at rocks and trees where there has been an epiphany of a God. And they haven't any priests, only these Holy Men. Being a Holy Man might happen to anyone. It starts with an epiphany of the God, a waking one like being struck by lightning, or in a dream. And the God lays a charge on you, and out you are driven to fulfil it. These Holy Men, of course, happen in a lot of lands where the people aren't really settled on the soil or haven't enough to eat. The Jews had them, and some of them wrote down the charges the God put on them. I've seen the Celtic ones, and they are very given to be holier than anyone else, and talk a lot about it. India is full of them. In Germany they are rare.

There are some Holy Men who eat no flesh, and some who live on nothing but fresh blood. There are some who may not touch women, and some who are, conveniently, driven by the God to sow their seed where they can. There

10

are some who wash and some who don't wash. The one I am going to talk about didn't wash.

We were sitting outside Rudi's Tavern one day, the last fine day of autumn. There was Aristarchos, prefect of a cavalry cohort, and Meno, from the Legion Headquarters, who was drowned in the Danube the following year. There was a lawyer called Polycleites, who didn't tell anyone why he had come up there on the edge of nowhere, though my father knew. We were, in fact, a little Greek club, all speaking Greek, and we were drinking beer and eating hot sausage; sometimes I think I lived on hot sausage in those days.

This Holy Man was worth looking at. He was well over six feet, and he had matted greasy yellow hair down to his waist. He had clothes on, and not all of them bother: a leather breech clout, and a scarlet cloak down to the hips in the German fashion, and that was new and clean.

He walked past the troops as if he didn't see them and they were glad to let him alone; some of these gentry have uncertain tempers. He came to the top of the bank, and he very carefully turned till he was looking straight into the eye of the sun. Then he put up his bare arm, and plucked something large and shining out of the empty air. That's not too difficult if you've been trained to it, as I have. It was too far off to see what. Then, whatever it was, he threw it straight at the sun. We followed its course in the air. Whether it was the wind or some God that held it I do not know, but I swear it changed its course, and it fell, quite gently, on to our table. It didn't even spill anyone's beer. We looked at it. It didn't roll. It was a great piece of Amber, twice the size of your two clenched fists. A king's ransom.

'Generous, isn't he?' said Aristarchos.'Oh, no, he's coming for it. You can smell him from here.'

You could too. Over he came, and he sat down at the table, pushing in between the two soldiers and opposite me. I felt

11

a bit of a devil, so as he sat down I made a few of the right passes and vanished the Amber, on to my lap under the table.

'Careful,' said Aristarchos. 'You'll be turned into a toad in another minute.'

However, the Holy Man didn't seem surprised. He just sat. There was no harm in being polite.

'Beer, Holy Sir,' I offered.

'Tiwaz has laid it on me. I drink no strong drink.' He had a strong northern accent. One of the tavern servants brought him a jug of water, and filled him a beaker.

He'd drawn it half an hour before out of the river. Never drink water unless you've seen it drawn; usually then you don't want to any more. The Holy Man must have had a stomach made of pottery; the water was darker than the beer.

He looked at the knives on the table. He leaned across and picked up Polycleites's knife. Polycleites opened his mouth and the other three of us all kicked him under the table. The Holy Man said in German, 'Iron, iron, iron,' three times, just like that. He spun the knife on the table. When it stopped the handle pointed to him, the point to me. He did the same thing with Aristarchos's knife, then with Meno's. Each time, the point of the knife looked straight at me. Last, he took my knife. He spun it. This time, the point came to him, the hilt to me. He drank again.

He looked at me. His blue eyes bored into my black. After a while he looked away. He looked at my hair. At that time, it was still possible that I might follow my father in the Temple, and my hair and beard had been uncut since birth. My hair was as long as his, black and clean against his dirty yellow.

He asked, 'What is your name, Roman?'

I didn't feel like arguing about Romans and Greeks, they all looked alike to him, anyway. I said,

'I am Photinus.'

'Photan, Votan, Woden, Odin,' he repeated, trying out all the variants which the Germans used. Germans can't learn to speak Greek, their tongues are too short, and they had great difficulty with the initial *Ph* of my name, turning

12

it sometimes into a digamma, sometimes into a double *u* and sometimes a single *u*, sometimes dropping it altogether.

'And what is your name, Holy Sir?'

'I have no name.'

'How do men call you, then?'

'I have no name. Men call me Joy.'

He stood up. He had the Amber in his hand. I had not seen or felt him take it back. It worried me. I stood up with him. I did not want to, I just felt I would. Always, in the north, whatever I did, even when I must have been obeying the command of a God, I felt I was doing what I wished.

He went back to the quay. He stood where he had stood before, this time most carefully placing his back to the sun, so that his shadow fell straight before him. Again he flung the Amber straight up into the air, straight above his head, and the sun caught it and it shone so that we could all mark it and see it curve down into the waters of the Danube. There were a dozen legionaries who spent the next week, all day and every day, diving for it, but they never found it.

There were a lot of people watching, mostly German. Joy turned away from the river. I had been expecting him to go back across the ferry, but no, he walked away, across the German quarter. I followed him. I had to. We came to a place by the Carnuntum road where there was an oak tree in an open space.

When he stopped there were about thirty or forty Germans with us. Two had spades. Without a word they began to dig. They dug a grave, seven feet long and two feet wide. When it was about four feet deep, others came and spread a layer of brushwood and twigs in the bottom. There was a great heap of brushwood too that they left by the graveside.

Joy turned to me and said in quite beautiful Greek, with no trace of an accent:

'I go to my Hesperides. I go to renew my youth.'

Another German came forward with a long rope. Joy tied a noose in it and placed it round his own neck. It struck me that there was something wrong. Joy's vows were to Tiwaz. But hanging was how you sacrificed to Wude, the

13

Wind God; you hanged the victim from a branch, wind about him, wind beneath him, the wind squeezed from his body.

Joy climbed into the tree. He sat astride a branch about ten feet up. He looked about him, and then threw me the end of the rope.

'Hold!' he said.

I passed the end of the rope around my body and braced myself. I felt the jerk as he jumped. The strain lasted a moment. Then a knife flashed and someone cut the rope. I turned to see. A dozen Germans held Joy's rigid body. The face was swollen, the tongue protruded.

I touched him. Born in Apollo's house, I knew where to touch him. In the temple, in the throat, there was the pulse of a day-old chick.

They laid him in the grave. Over him they heaped more brushwood. They covered all with a few inches of earth. We all went away.

Each day I went back at noon to the oak tree. The grave was untouched, the earth drying on the brushwood. On the ninth day the grave was open. In it was a layer of ash and charred twigs. There was no body alive or dead, burnt or unburnt. Where Joy was I did not know.

None of my friends ever mentioned again that struggle in the tavern. None of the Germans under the tree, many of them men I knew, ever mentioned it again. Otho never spoke of it at all. But he knew.

3

There was just one other thing wrong with Vindabonum. Or right, depending on your point of view. There were an awful lot of men, gentlemen, that is, and not many ladies. There were plenty for the legionaries and the Germans, I mean, but not so many that you could really associate with. There were a few local gentry, if you had a low standard for gentrydom, and some of the auxiliary and legionary officers were married, but too many of these had picked up their

14

wives in the fish-market when they were in the ranks. So the really attractive ones were rare, and those honey pots drew a lot of wasps.

The effect of this was not altogether what you might imagine. There wasn't really anything for either men or women to do a great deal of the time. Nothing for the women, except to run small houses with cheap slaves. Very little for officers in third-rate regiments on garrison duty. A few, like Aristarchos, would go out to find something to do, and they didn't stay long, even if they lived. But even that kind of garrison life entails a fair amount of detached duty at isolated posts and all kinds of chances to get out into the country. This didn't mean that the ladies were more accessible. It only meant that the ladies made all the running.

There were a fair variety of doctors in Vindabonum. There were half a dozen Greeks, a couple of Jews, and a whole crowd of Germans, who might be anything from properly trained priests to witches hung with charms. Any of them was perfectly capable of looking after broken arms or sprains or the occasional stab wounds. After every tavern brawl, one of the Greeks, who had been in Egypt and was a specialist, a real specialist recognised by the military, would have a spate of business relieving skull fractures. Most of these were due to Rudi's chucker-out, a man called Donar. He was something of a mystery. He sounded like a northerner, and had been working as a smith, but had thrown this up on a sudden in the autumn to work for Rudi. He was not tall, but burly, very muscular, and he had a fine crop of red hair and beard.

So for routine medicine the town was well provided. But when my father arrived, and they realised that he wasn't going to practise, in spite of all his prestige, the local doctors adopted him as a kind of elder statesman of medicine. The way they showed this was quite simple. When they got anything that was quite incurable like visitations of boils or sores, they would pass it on to him as a superior operator. Once Milo, the trepanning specialist, even sent around a skull fracture he wasn't keen on, just alive, with the brains

15

oozing out. Of course the man died. Luckily the family chose to believe it wasn't my father who killed him, but the bouncing around in the ox wagon from door to door. So they sued Milo, and Polycleites was drunk again that day and lost the case for him. Nobody ever tried to sue Rudi, or Donar.

A lot of other odd cases arrived. There were facial tics and cases of paralysis and just plain madness. Most of them came from citizens, not from Germans. Those were probably afraid that they'd have to pay. Once my father found he was practising again, he began to charge on a swingeing scale.

'Patients don't trust you if they don't pay,' he would tell me. 'If they want to get well, they have to do something about it themselves. The only thing they can do is pay. So I make them pay.'

He would never have me around when he was dealing with these cases, but there was one winter evening when he began to explain his methods.

'There's not much you can do to tics, and so on. I just ask them how it got started. They become so interested in telling me about it that they forget to tic. First of all they have short spells of not twitching. Next they get to the stage when they don't twitch at all in the surgery. Then they get so excited they stop twitching an hour before they get here, in sheer anticipation, and they forget to start twitching again till a couple of hours after they leave.

'There are other things, too. Do you know how these ailments start? Take Julia Scapella, for instance. How much older do you think old Scapellus is than she? Twenty years? There he is, senior centurion of the Legion. Not only that, it makes him chief of staff for six thousand infantry, four cavalry regiments, and heaven knows how many minor posts and storehouses. Think of the pickings.

'Well, now he's static, he begins to think he ought to have a wife to suit his dignity, none of these early marriages with fishwives for him, and off he sends to a broker in Rome, probably the one he got his name through. Up the girl comes, never seen him before, doesn't know a thing, and it comes as a bit of a shock. Then she begins to get boils

16

on her . . . well, she gets boils. So he begins that round of staff visits, and they get longer and longer, and she begins to appreciate the good things in life she's missing. And now she's looking for treatment. The treatment is obvious. But not to her.'

It was to me, though, and it didn't take long to begin it, not with that bit of inside knowledge, and what I could easily pick up about Scapellus's roster of visits. Not long, either, before Julia was paying a good fee for the complete cure of her boils, and I am pleased to say that my father made no attempt to avoid splitting it two ways. But this was what started all the trouble, in the spring.

4

It was one of the nights Otho came to dinner. He often came to dinner, or we went to him, as he had rented us the house next door to his, close to the west gate. This was a quiet affair, not like the big parties my father often used to give in those days for the other doctors, and people of better standing. There were just the three of us, and we were discussing the general state of trade.

'So what are we in business here for?' Otho asked. He knew more about the situation than anyone else on the river, which was why we employed him.

'We trade for timber and hides, and wax. Some slaves, ragged savages, some furs, ragged pelts from moth-eaten bears (I will tell you some day how the mother moth finds her way back to her nest in the moving bear). Marcomen bring them down to the ferry, ragged Marcomen. We pay them in pots, wine, silver. Good round silver, beautiful shining silver. We pay them in coins, silver coins. They don't want coin because they want to spend it, it's just that when silver comes in coin they know how pure it is. If those oafs in Rome knew how much trouble they cause each time they debase it. They know all about that, out in Germany. "We want old denarii," they tell me. "Two-horse denarii, one of

17

those or two of the new kind." They want wine . . . wine . . . wine . . .' I filled his cup.

'They want wine, red wine. They want pottery, red Samian pottery, the lovely red shine of the glaze. And glass, too, glass from Campania, glass they want more than gold. Gold? What do they want with gold? A little piece of gold pays for a lot of hides, and there it is, a little piece. But for the same hides you can have enough silver to make into the mount for a drinking horn or a morse to fasten your cloak with. And if the silver you start off with is coin, two-horse denarii that you melt down, then you know you've got good silver.'

'Silver as a raw material for an industry,' mused my father.

'But there is something that comes down, but not often, and for that I always give silver. It glows . . . it shines . . .'

'Amber,' I breathed. 'Perhaps once a month, perhaps less often you see that. High profit, perhaps, but not what you'd call an important article of trade.'

'Not now, not now.' I gave Otho more wine, it was worth staying in for, to hear this kind of thing.

'Sixty, seventy years ago, this was a great place for the Amber trade. Those days, the Romans came up from Aquileia, up the Marc River, to trade for Amber with the Marcomen. There were real Marcomen there, then, my fathers. The Amber came down, Amber by the wagon load, think of it, by the wagon load, red glowing Amber. They paid for the Amber, and then they paid our wagoners to take it down to Aquileia, and then we sold them the oxen out of the wagons, all thin and tired from the journey, as fat stock. Ah, those were the fine days . . .'

'How did they end?' I asked.

'Herman came. First he beat the Romans up in the north, three legions he cut up and not one word heard of them again. We had our Good King then, my grandfather Maroboduus. Herman defeated him, drove him out. All our fine warriors dead, our women raped, our children sold, all our nobles driven out, scattered, dead, dead. The Good King, he died in Ravenna. They made us all citizens because we hated

18

Herman and so did the Romans, but the Marcomen are ruled now by renegades, people of low birth. And Herman and his Thuringians joined with the Cat King, and they hold all the centre of the great plain, and all the Amber they make goes through their hands and through the Thuringians, and to the Rhine. And it is paying the two sets of duty on it, to the Cat King and to the Thuringians, that makes Amber so expensive. But if we could open the road east of the Cat men, and bring Amber down without paying the dues, if someone could go to the Kings of the Amber Road in the north, why then, think of the profits . . .'

We thought. It was enticing.

'Could you get anyone to go?' my father asked.

'I've got someone,' said Otho. 'Two men. They know the way to the north and I can trust them. They will take a little silver, but mostly they will go to meet people and find out the way. Occa will go.'

I knew Occa. He was a sergeant-major in Aristarchos's regiment. I had heard he was due for a long leave.

'And the other?'

'Donar.'

A chucker-out? I stopped thinking about the scheme, there was nothing in it, nothing at all.

We gave Otho more wine, and left him crying into his cups that he couldn't find anyone of spirit willing to go, no one of intelligence or learning. He kept looking at me, and I kept ignoring him. There was nothing in the plan at all. Only wind.

5

Two days later it was the first fine day of spring. I had nothing to do, exiles usually haven't. I had watched old Scapellus ride out on a long tour down river, all the posts to Carnuntum. That would keep him out of the way for a few nights, and I had already arranged how to occupy them. Then I had a work-out at the cavalry gymnasium. I had been having a few lessons with the cavalry sword, the long springy one. There's quite a different technique with it. As I came out of the barracks I saw two off-duty legionaries. I wouldn't have noticed them if they hadn't been so obviously taking notice of me.

I went off to Rudi's tavern; I was peckish after the exercise, and it was so sunny I sat on a bench outside sheltered from the wind, and ordered beer and hot sausages. It was a bit early and while the girl was getting the sausages heated up I ate a couple of salt herrings out of the barrel; they came down from the north too. After a while I looked across the street, and the two legionaries were there, not doing anything but standing against the wall of the house opposite and looking at me. Just looking. They were the same two. Their look made me feel a bit uncomfortable. After a bit, I called the girl and had her move me indoors by the fire. At least it didn't look as if they had chased me away.

It was more cheerful inside. I gossiped with Rudi's number one wife. He made the best of both worlds; he told the Romans that polygamy was a German custom, and to the Germans he said that was how the Romans lived at home in the south. Then she chivvied the number three wife, who had just brought me the hot sausages, to go and look after two new customers. I looked over, and they were the same two legionaries asking for beer. They bought half a pint each, the cheapest kind, and one of them made an entry on his tablets as if he was keeping account of his expenses. Then they sat nursing their pots and looking at me.

I looked back. They weren't very formidable in themselves, rather mild in fact. I knew them both by sight. That one looked after living-out permits for legionaries with native wives in the German quarter. The other was with the quartermaster, dealing with arrowheads and other warlike expendable stores. Not the kind of men to beat anybody up, but conscientious, pedantic, reliable, just the kind to use for following. Literate too, could write a report afterwards.

In this position, how do you get rid of your follower? Easy, I thought, I've never known the soldier yet who'll pass up

20

a free meal. When I finished my sausage, I called over the number three wife.

'Those two gentlemen over there by the door, nearly through their beer. Get them a good big dish of hot sausages, bread, onions. Any radishes? Good, those too. And a quart apiece of best beer, the strong black stuff. Don't mention my name, and keep the change.'

I suppose she thought I was mad, but that didn't matter. She was glad of the tip, since she was saving to buy Rudi another wife so that she'd no longer get all the kicks.

As soon as she got the tray over to their table I got up and slipped out past her. There was enough on that tray to keep them busy for a quarter of an hour at least, even if they gobbled like pigs, and I was barely a furlong from Otho's house, which had a side door into ours. But as I came to the gate, I looked behind me, and there they were on the street corner looking back at me.

When I got into the house, I found Otho was not alone. Donar was there, and another man. If Donar was burly, this one was cubic, the same measurement tall and wide and deep. It was Occa. I don't know what his calvary regiment rode on; elephants, I should think. He had scars all up his arms; rumour says that he had once tackled a bear single handed, and it was the bear that ran away. Looking at him you could believe it. He was rubbing pig fat into his face. Donar was putting a last edge on a sword with a strop. Otho was weighing out silver pieces into bags, fourteen pounds in a bag.

I stopped and looked at them.

'Off this afternoon?' I asked.

'Tonight,' said Occa.

'Over the wall,' said Donar.

'Over the wall in the dark?' I asked. It was fairly easy, if nobody spotted you; the town wall was one side of Otho's courtyard. 'Why not just walk out of the gates in the morning?'

The three Germans looked at me in a pitying way, as if I had missed the point of something obvious.

'Nonsense,' said Occa. 'No story ever started by stealthily slipping through the gates unguarded in day undiminished.'

'Have you no piety?' asked Donar. 'No sense of achievement? A feat at the first gives the Gods greater glory.'

The Germans speak like that when they want to be formal. I could talk their language fairly well by now, and I thought I might try my hand at ceremony one day. At that moment I was content with saying, 'Watch out for your necks on the other side.' And I went up to my room. I had a couple of hours' sleep, and then I began to dress for my visit to Julia. I was still thinking about Donar sneaking out of the town in the dark, probably leaving behind a handful of bad debts and a couple of sweethearts in the family way.

I had some dinner in my room, and then I set out for Julia's. I crossed our courtyard, and the gate keeper opened up for me. I stepped out into the dark street and stood for a moment with the open gate at my back. I looked about. In a sheltered alcove a little way along there were two men standing. They were not in the least concerned with keeping out of the moonlight, but only with keeping out of the wind. They were easy to recognise, even at that distance. As I looked at the two watchers, someone seized my arm from behind and pulled me back into the courtyard.

'Have you no sense?' asked Aristarchos. 'Haven't you seen them?'

'Seen them?' I tried to be reasonable. 'They've been on my trail all day. I paid for their dinner, but they didn't eat it.'

'Two of my lads did. They told me about it. Do you know who they are?'

'Yes. Two clerks from Headquarters Century.'

'Scapellus's century.'

'So? Who's afraid of that weedy pair? I didn't even bring a sword out with me. I don't think either of them has handled a weapon since they did recruit drill.'

'No,' said Aristarchos very slowly, as if he were speaking to a foreigner, or to a child. 'No, not that kind of man. You don't use that kind of man to kill. I don't, anyway, and that's my job, and it's Scapellus's job too, and he's been at it a lot longer than I have. No, that kind of man you use for following and watching, because they do it so well. You use others for killing. I know I would, so Scapellus will.'

'Do you think that illiterate squarehead can get the better of Greeks like us?' Scapellus was half German, they said, and the best part of his education he'd got in the barrack-room. Aristarchos was sounding a bit scornful, so there was no harm in buttering him up a bit, even if he was only a Thracian with a thick accent.

'I don't know what they're watching for, and anyway, Scapellus hasn't any civil jurisdiction . . . has he . . . ? I've got a week before he comes back, and I never knew a quartermaster who couldn't be bribed.'

'Let us look at this in detail,' said Aristarchos smoothly, very much one Greek to another. 'First of all, they're watching for you to call on Julia. You've been seen before, you know. All Scapellus wants to do is catch you on the premises. Secondly, you haven't got a week. Scapellus didn't go to Carnuntum, he only went as far as the tenth milecastle on the river, and he's coming back by dawn. I did the ration documents for the escort, so that's how I know. And thirdly, it isn't only that pair watching. When Scapellus comes back tomorrow, he's going to find you trussed up and waiting for him.'

'Now, now,' I said, 'that's going a bit far. Julia wouldn't let me down like that. Nor the house slaves either, they're under her thumb.'

'House slaves don't come into it. They're under lock and key. So is Julia, and she's got that Syrian, Publiolus's wife, to chaperone her. You didn't know you'd been seen there too, did you? And then there's Manlius's wife, in our regiment, to chaperone them, and that's how I know. So look, Photinus, don't go up the street tonight, because a couple of those boys will hustle you in through that door whether you like it or not. And if you don't go up the street tonight, walk carefully the next few days. If Scapellus comes home and finds the trap sprung and empty, he might come calling.'

'So what do I do now?'

'Sit tight and stay indoors for a bit. Now it's clouding over, I'm going to run for it. If they let Scapellus think I tipped you off I'm for it.'

He slid through the gate into the dark. I knew that when he had been farther down the river, he had had a bad reputation as a horse thief. Now he moved like it.

I closed the gate and thought hard. If Julia was crying her heart out with the Syrian, there was no knowing what they were plotting between them. I might not have Scapellus round at once, but I'd probably have Publiolus at the door first thing in the morning. How long was I to stay indoors? A week? A month? Even if I did stay inside, there was nothing to stop Scapellus and his bullies from pushing the door in. And once husbands began to think over Julia's troubles — nothing could hide Scapellus coming back five days early — there was no knowing who might be coming round.

So what was I to do? I could hardly leave Vindabonum; I was, however you looked at it, under arrest. Anywhere else I could just have got out of town, just like I did at Ostia, when the husband came back, and after that unfortunate affair with the pimp in Alexandria, and as for Tyre, I never thought I'd find a Levantine who'd play with my dice. But in each of those places I had a ship to get back to and comrades who were at least as deep in it as I was. But there was no travelling about the Empire for me, with a pack of vengeful husbands all eager to put me under arrest. I was trapped, with the river at my back. Then it struck me. A river is a road, water is a way. I slipped through the internal gate into Otho's courtyard and went into his office. Otho and Donar looked at me curiously. Occa was greasing his boots.

'Don't go for an hour or so,' I told them. 'I'm coming with you.'

Germany

1

I went straight back to my own room and called Ursa.

'Quick,' I told her in German. 'Get me some German clothes. Shirt, trews, short cloak, sandals. Quick.'

Out of the cupboard I heaved a leather bag with a shoulder strap, made for a pack mule once but better this way. In it I put my best sky-blue silk tunic and a spare pair of sandals. I had a few pieces of silver handy, but after what I'd heard I didn't think it worth taking gold. I looked round and found one or two pieces of silver plate, old-fashioned embossed stuff. Then I took a leather water bottle with a strap, one I used to use out hunting.

If I were going north to meet the Amber Kings, I thought, I needed a king's clothes. I had a helmet, no, not a helmet, a cap of boiled leather, all covered and patterned with gold leaf, and this I put in, and a cuirass to match, for show not for war, soft leather and gold wire. These had come from the east somewhere, long ago, and had caught my fancy. I took a sword, the first I learnt to use, a Kopis, pointed, curved, one edge razor-sharp, the other finger-thick, blunt, the bone breaker, a fine hilt, but a plain scabbard. The general effect was of something meant for real use, but I knew well the metal wasn't of the best.

I was writing a letter to my father when Ursa came back with the clothes. She had a complete German suit, red woollen shirt, and red and yellow checked trousers. It was unworn, and a perfect fit; she must have started making it for me weeks before. Trousers are funny things to wear. You

25

can always feel them on your legs. It takes you a long time to get used to riding a horse in them, the cloth spoils the contact with the beast's side.

She didn't bring me a German cloak. They are short. She brought me my own long grey horseman's cloak, down to my heels.

'This is good for blanket, sleep in it,' she told me. I finished the letter to my father. I stood up to go. Ursa threw her arms round my neck.

'Rejoice,' she said; she said it in Greek, it was one of the few words she knew, then in German:

'Rejoice. Joy goes with you. Joy awaits you. Joy sends you on. Rejoice.'

I went down into our courtyard on the soft German sandals. Hobnails are no use out there beyond the Frontier, there are no paved roads. I went through the postern into Otho's courtyard, right under the town wall. The others were there, and a crowd of slaves, all talking at once.

'When do we start?' I asked Occa.

'Now,' he said. 'Somebody's gone to get the ladder.'

This shows what a state the river frontier was like then, you could build houses right up against city walls, inside anyway. One of Otho's slaves brought a ladder and set it against the wall. There was a sentry on top, walking about.

'What about him?' I asked.

'He won't see anything,' said Otho. I wondered how much that had cost. It wasn't only paying the sentry, the firm had probably had to pay the Guard Commander as well, and almost certainly somebody in the Legion Headquarters had a hand in the purse.

'How many has he been paid not to see?' I asked. I didn't want Scapellus over the river after us first thing.

'Any number,' said Otho. 'Up you go.'

I hate ladders on land. It's one thing climbing on a ship, but quite another when you only have the hard ground to fall on. I followed Donar up the ladder clinging on as tight as I could. Occa kept pushing me. We got on to the top. The sentry turned his back on us. Otho shouted up,

26

'Have you got the rope?'

Donar threw one end of a rope down, and half a dozen of Otho's slaves tailed on to the end of it. Then one by one we slid down the other side of the wall. We made enough noise to wake Morpheus, especially as each of us was carrying two fourteen-pound bags of silver coin.

We walked down a path to the river side.

'How do we cross it?' I asked. 'The ferry stopped hours ago.'

'You've been at sea,' Occa told me. 'You're going to row.'

If I had, I'd not rowed, I'd sailed like a gentleman. Out to Tyre in furs and honey, Tyre to Alexandria in cedarwood, Alexandria to Ostia in wheat, and a trooping run home. One year at sea, it showed me the world. I didn't want to sink to rowing.

It wasn't as bad as that. There was a small, illegal boat hidden in the reeds just where any legionary would have looked for it – more expense, I thought, and all for sentiment's sake. I was able to let her go down with the current and land up on the other side of a bend, where a man had been showing a lantern at intervals. I suppose it was another of Otho's contacts. He had three horses for us, those small scrubby things, and a great luxury, saddles, which were just coming in in those days. Most people out in the north just rode on blankets thrown over the horses' backs. We mounted and off we went. I was in the middle. The others seemed to know where we were going.

We rode for days. Some people talk as if the lands outside the Empire are quite different. In fact, it's just the same at first. For a couple of days we went along stretches of agger, roads laid by the army in Domitian's campaign ten years before, unused since and now breaking up under weather and time, not wear. All the country was like that. The people were the same as on our side of the river, the clothes were the same, the language, the houses, the food. But it was all a bit shabbier and second-rate. The houses weren't as clean as the German houses around the walls of Vindabonum, and that means they were foul.

After the first few days we didn't pass many houses. When I came back that way I began to realise how skilfully Occa had planned his march to take us out of people's sight and earshot. Usually we rose at dawn and rode off at once. We would stop at noon and rest the horses and eat, and after an hour or two set off again till sunset. We had dried meat and twice-baked bread with us. Once or twice Occa went off with his bow and got a deer, though it was really out of the season, and we called at farms and bartered the meat and hide for carrots and cabbages that had been stored through the winter.

We followed the Marcomen's river, a little east of north through the empty hills. One day, a little before sunset, we came out of the wood, the scrubby patchy stuff you get near a river, into an open space. In the middle there was an oak, a very old oak, dead, blasted and scarred by lightning. Occa stopped and held up his hand.

'The God has been here,' he said.

'That was a long time ago,' I told him.

'Yes, seven years ago, in July,' he replied. I had not realised that his knowledge of the way was so exact or so recent. He went on, 'There is something new. Can a dead tree put forth a new shoot, or the dry rock a living branch? It is new that the oak should sent out ash, or the dull rock smite as a smith. From here it looks like a splinter, hanging vertical from the trunk, but it is new. Do as I do.'

As I watched Occa took out his water bottle and poured a few drops out on the ground, as a libation. This was mere politeness, a greeting to the sky-god. As we rode forward behind him we saw that the ground was scattered with horse skulls and bits of faded cloth held down by stones. Beneath the tree was the skeleton of a horse, whole, only a few months dead.

Donar stopped me a dozen yards from the tree. Occa kicked his heels into his horse and rode forward, hard, and as he passed the tree he grasped the spear shaft and pulled it. He let it go just in time to avoid sliding off the horse's back. The spear did not move.

28

Then Donar rode forward. From where I sat I could see the muscles of his arm and back strain as he pulled, but again the spear did not move. I thought of riding sedately past, uncertain of whether they would appreciate my meddling with their German rites, but Donar shouted to me to come on and have a pull.

I clapped my heels into the horse's ribs and went full tilt at the tree. I grabbed at the shaft, calling on Apollo to let me grasp it, even if I never moved it. My hands felt the smooth shaft, jerked it, slipped a little. I had the spear.

The two Germans shouted, a paean, a warcry, a great ululation. Without looking back we rode away, miles away up the river, none of us speaking till we reached what looked like a good camping place for the night. I sat on my saddle, while the others hobbled the horses and turned them to graze, and I looked at the spear. It was the usual long iron head on a six foot ash shaft. It had not been in the weather very long, perhaps six months at the most, and there was only a very thin coating of rust. I'm not sure it hadn't been greased before it was left. I got some ash and some sand and I began to clean the metal.

Donar and Occa came and sat by me and told me how it must have happened.

'It is our custom, all over Germany,' said Donar, 'that when a man is going out on some desperate journey from which there is no returning, if he goes to join the cavalry, or to do a murder, or to his death . . .'

'Or to his marriage.' Occa, in middle age, was a bachelor.

'. . . he will take a weapon, a knife or an axe, or a spear, and he will thrust it into a tree . . .'

'And he will make an offering to the God, don't forget the offering. This one made the horse sacrifice.'

That was the most magnificent and most expensive sacrifice of all, and this had been the most costly: a mare.

'Then every man who passes must try to draw the weapon out of the tree, and only the man for whom the God intends it will be able to take it. That spear was meant for you, Photinus.'

The rust was almost all gone. I showed the ferrule just below the head to Donar.

'What are these marks below the crosspiece?' For it had a crosspiece like a boar spear, and that was not usual.

They both looked at it closely. I know that many people think that the Germans have no writing, but I have the best of reasons for knowing better. Certainly you cannot write German words in Greek or Latin letters, that would be against all reason, but there is a way of writing German in German letters, which are called Runes. This was the first time I had seen Runes, and in my innocence I thought that any German could read them. This time I heard nothing to disturb my delusion, for Occa took one glance and said,

'That means Joy. Joy left that spear. Joy left you his spear. That is why he sought you at the ferry.'

A few days later I asked Donar to take his punches and strike my name into the iron on the other side of the socket. So now Votan lies for ever in the iron with Joy. But only Donar could read it, for in those days in the North every man made his own runes.

2

A few days later we were coming out of the land of no people, the bare mountains, into a land of scattered farms and shepherds. And then, in a few more days, the farms were more frequent, the population thickened, concentrated, condensed almost, out of a cloud of precarious settlers into a vortex, a constellation of permanent farms, hamlets, villages almost, little clusters of houses and barns.

We came to the farm of one of Occa's clansmen, Haro, a man of power and influence in the region. He was, I had been told, Otho's agent among the Marcomen, but he said that Otho was his agent among the Romans. He came himself and unbarred the gates of his stockade – they had been shut specially for the purpose – to let us in. The farmyard was built up feet above the plain on the dung and rubbish of generations. Inside the stockade, the main farmhouse was a great hall, the frame of whole trees, the walls filled with wattle and daub, the roof thatched with wheat straw. It was twenty paces long, inside, and ten wide. The door was in the middle of the long side, and the hearth at one end, sure sign that Haro had only lately dispensed with the company of his cows at night. They now slept, in winter, in the huts scattered around the yard. At least in some of the huts; we three were put into one, and bidden be ready for a feast that night.

There was a group of women around a fire outside one hut, and I went over and asked for some hot water. They sent the youngest to bring it over, and she set down the pot by the door, and walked away with serious face, steady and erect like a grown-up, she hoped, though it was obvious that one word would have set her off giggling, and scurrying back.

We washed the dust away, and I put on my best tunic. Then we sat outside the door and watched the other guests arrive, big proud men, chiefs with their war bands, or at least the pick of their war bands. They all went into the hall. At last, Occa decided dignity would let us appear, and in we went. This was the first time I had been the guest of a German, other than Otho with his Spanish butler and his Syrian cook, and his nearly Roman dining-room with its three tables and couches. This room had three tables, too, one across the width of the hall farthest from the door, and the others at right angles down the sides. Haro met us and offered us that sweet Spanish wine, which those Germans are so keen on as an appetiser. It was very precious there, so no more than one glass was offered, and that a very small one. There was not so much as an eggspoonful of sea water or resin there to blend in it, so I was not sorry that the main drink of the evening was to be beer.

When the wine was drunk with the usual exchange of healths, we guests of honour went to sit on the long benches behind the top table, our backs to the hearth, our faces to a brazier. I moved to the seat to which Haro waved me, and as I sat down, he bellowed, as if introducing the only stranger:

31

'Photinus the Greek, from the sea and the islands. Far has he travelled, to the islands of the spices. He left behind comfort to sleep in the forest, left behind women, silks, sauces and silver. He overcame Joy to come on this journey, Greek vowed to his God he goes to the Northlands. Spear on shoulder he rides through the mountains, over the plains to the Kings of the Amber.'

I thought this a bit unwise if we were supposed to be going in secret, but Occa assured me that we had only the Cat King to fear, and that all present were Marcomen and Quadi, enemies of the Cat people. So I sat down, and watched what we would have for supper. I must say there was more order and ceremony at this banquet than at any other barbarian feast I ever went to. Each of us was given a pair of silver mounted drinking horns – on the top table, that is; farther down they brought their own. The retainers were crammed together; at least we had room to move our elbows.

First the servants brought salt fish, to give us a thirst, and then filled the horns, one with barley beer, the other with mead. After the fish, gross hunks of roast meat were placed on the table, with loaves of rye bread. My neighbour, with a great effort at courtesy, cut me thick slabs of pig and deer mixed together. He wore a cloak of wolf pelts, with a wolf's head hanging down behind. On a golden chain round his neck were wolf's teeth, dozens of them. He made a sport, he told me, a trade, a livelihood, of wolf hunting, with spear, with bow, with trap, even with poison, winter and summer. His own name he himself had almost forgotten. Everyone now called him Wolf. I could no more applaud his pursuit of wolves than I could approve of Occa's attack on the bear, but in his name I found an omen. He had a healthy respect for his wolves, in spite of the fifty tails sewn on the hem of his cloak.

'Only two good things about wolves. They make good cloaks and they can't climb trees. Bear climbs trees, but not wolf. If you ever want to cheat them, get up a tree. Stay there. Stay there till they go. Hours, days, maybe, but stay there.'

His main topic, that night, was the indignity of having

to come, at Haro's insistence, unarmed into the hall. He proudly showed a scar across his scalp, from front to back.

'I got that at a feast, up with the Thuringians, big man he was, good fellow, know him well. Got some of the best wolf hunting this side of the great forest. I'll take you up there one day, great sport. What? The scar? Yes, well, that was after the dinner, we can't remember why, but he hit me with a bench. No swords, but it didn't stop us fighting.'

'If it had been a sword,' my other neighbour observed – his name was Lothar, and, he was delighted to tell me, he had been across the border twice, once on a cattle raid and once into Carnuntum to market – 'if it had been a sword, where would you be now?'

He rolled up his shirt to show a fine scar across his stomach.

'*That* was a sword. It was my wedding feast and my brand new brother-in-law did it. It kept me in bed three weeks – quiet, Wolf, we haven't all got minds like yours. But there, if we'd all been hit on the heads with benches . . . Here, our guest's plate is empty. Pass the beef – no, try this, a real local delicacy. What? Oh, bulls' testicles, raw.'

'Perhaps he doesn't eat them,' said Wolf in an interested way. 'Oh, yes, he does, though. All right, they always taste like that at first, really. Try some more mead. Go on, drain it! Boy! More mead!'

The mead finished me. The next thing I knew I was struggling out into the courtyard. I don't know how I managed to reach fresh air without disgracing myself. Wolf was at my elbow, not jeering as I feared but bitterly regretting his own lack of capacity.

'Small bladder, that's my trouble, always has been. I can stand up to the liquor itself, strong head I've got, but once over the gallon and a half, out I've got to come. That's right, boy, get it up, get rid of it, you'll feel better then. Only good thing about the south, there's not so much bulk to wine. All right? Let's get back then, there's still some cold roast pork left, and plenty of crackling. There, there, get it up. I thought you were finished for a moment, but . . . here's some water, clear your taste. What, *over* your head? Are you sure? Well, all right then. No, better not go to lie down, it isn't etiquette. Back we go, I'll make sure they don't press you to any more. Takes a bit of getting used to, I suppose. Here we grow up on it. Just sit still a bit. Lothar! pass me the pork.'

I only wish now that I could recover from a drinking bout the way I could then. A slab of rye bread and a draught of beer, not the rich dark stuff I had been drinking, but the ordinary thin bitter brew, well beer we used to call it, and I was able to watch what was happening again. There was a minstrel now, standing by the fire and singing away, some long involved song about a hero who was killing a dragon, very slowly. For line after monotonous line the sword slid past one scale after another. I must have looked bored, for Haro leant across and said to me:

'Good, isn't he? But what does Greek sound like?'

Now, when people say that to you, as they often do abroad, it's no use saying something like 'No, thank you', because they always want a translation. I had to think of something to suit the company. This was hardly the time or the place for Sappho. Homer, in contrast, was both too near and too far away from them in spirit. I took something which would show them both how near the Greek mood could come to theirs, and at the same time how foreign to them was its precision. I spoke the two lines of the epitaph on the Spartans at Thermopylae:

Go, tell the Spartans, thou who passest by,
That here obedient to their laws we lie.

'And what does it mean?' they all shouted together.

'Give me some quiet and I will tell you,' I said. Now was the moment to see if I really could make verse in German. Wolf, with excellent aim after the amount of beer he had taken, threw a mutton bone at the bard, who fell into the brazier, and while some people poured beer over him to put the flames out, and others poured beer into him to revive him, Haro passed me his harp. I tried a few chords. It was not too different from a lyre, provided I only used it to beat out the rhythm. Anyone brought up on hexameters should find German verse easy, I thought, drunk or sober. Whether I was right or wrong is not for me to say, but as far as I remember this is what I sang:

Men went to battle, there was no returning.
Go tell in Sparta, low burns our pyre.
We were three hundred, they ten times ten thousand.
From sea to mountain set we the shield wall.
Over the hill flank came the betrayer.
Broken the shield wall, bloody the sea shore.
Our Kings commanded us, bear no shield back again.
Men went to battle, there was no returning.

It didn't leave a dry eye in the place. Men were weeping for their lost comrades, for their own lost youth, for the days when they too might have stood to die in a shield wall, not gone home as soon as they were outnumbered, like sensible married men. To break the ocean of sobbing, Haro shouted:

'Bring a cloak, put down a cloak, let's have a cloak and a couple of them on it.'

Two of the retainers came forward with a cloak, an old thing, stained and torn, but a big one, a horseman's cloak like mine. They spread it on the floor between the brazier and the top table. Out of the confusion at the bottom of the hall, two men were pushed, half reluctant, to stand on the cloak. Each had a shield, one daubed with an eagle, one with a bear. Somebody brought them their swords.

You may not have seen a German sword, not to handle. They are different from ours. Ours have a point; the legionary's is short and stiff, the cavalry trooper's sword is long and springy, but each has a point, and you use them on the move, putting all your own fifteen stone or the speed of your horse behind it, to drive through leather or mail.

Germans, on the contrary, like to fight standing still. They depend on the strength of their arms and the weight of their weapons to do the damage, and so their swords are two-edged, but rounded at the tip, not pointed. The sword is always long, four fingers broad at the hilt, and two fingers at the tip. Down from hilt to tip, on each side, there runs a groove, some say to collect the blood, some say to make the blade stronger, some say because the blades were always made that way. The hilts they hang round with charms and rings, and they usually keep them covered with little leather bags to protect the finery.

These two men, Bear-shield and Bird-shield, stood on the cloak. The shields were of limewood, covered with leather, and strengthened with iron. The fight they made was nothing you'll ever see at the games; it was too slow, no audience would ever pay to see it. They stood face to face, on the cloak, a pace apart. When Haro shouted 'Start!' each began to move crabwise to his left, keeping his shield between himself and his opponent. Then Bear-shield struck, a wild slashing blow, and the other turned it on the edge of his shield. They crabbed again, and then Bird-shield had a cut, the weight of that long blade far forward. He leaned forward too far, and almost overbalanced, and I waited for Bear-shield to go for the back of the knee and hamstring him, but no, the idiot stood aside and let his opponent recover. Then they went around again, and Bear-shield had a go, and again the blow was turned. They went on like that, turn and turn about to cut, for what seemed to me like hours, always careful to keep their feet on the cloak.

After a few dozen of these blows, the shields were pretty tattered. Bear-man looked at his shield in disgust, and flung it behind him. It seemed this had to be done when you were due to receive a blow, not when you were about to deal one, and your opponent then had to throw his shield away too. Bird-man wasn't very pleased, obviously, but he struck, and though Bear-man swayed back, the tip of the sword caught him on the ear. The blood ran down his neck, slowly. A number of the audience were down on their hands and knees at the edge of the cloak. Everything was quiet, and the torch flames made everything dance in silence. Then Bear-man had a slash, Bird-man parried with the flat of his blade, but the other with a flick of his wrist changed the direction of his cut in mid-air, and chopped sideways along the Bird-man's arm. The blood spouted down his fingers on to the cloak, and the kneelers shouted and Haro shouted and we all shouted and the two swordsmen embraced and rubbed each other's wounds with the trinkets from their swords. It seemed that drawing first blood didn't mean you'd won; but the man who first dropped blood on the cloak lost.

There were a number of fights after that, and a fair amount of betting. I did well on one fight between a big local man, and a small stranger who was left-handed; I reasoned that the right-hander would be put off, while the left-hander probably fought right-handed men every week. He did too, and won in about three or four cuts.

Then there were a pair of elderly men, rather fat, who were so inept that we just threw mutton bones at them and laughed them off the cloak. They were followed by a grudge fight, in earnest, between the local expert, who elected to fight without a shield and take the first stroke, and a novice who was to keep his shield – there was much bad blood in this one. However, while the expert was circling for his second blow, and that, I am sure, would have been the end of the novice, he put his foot on a mutton bone and down he went. He turned the ankle, and couldn't get up, and there he lay while some argued over the bets, and a gaggle of local doctors talked over whether the poultice would be better mixed with pig's blood or with bull's urine. None of them bothered to look at the patient, so I did. It didn't take a moment to feel what was wrong with that joint, not to anyone with my training. The clever thing was to do something about it. I tipped the wink to Donar, who stood ready to hold the shoulders.

The problem was finding the leg under about seven layers of wrappings, without alarming the patient. How would you do it? Just a bit of skill, and you'd never believe the things I took out of those wrappings. Mutton bones, chicken legs, a drinking horn, all with a flow of more or less obscene patter that got the sufferer and everyone else into fits of laughter. When I had the boot off, even some of the Quadi remarked

37

on the smell, but I merely slipped in 'Venite' as a signal, and Donar pulled and I twisted and the expert howled and the bone came right.

Then I wrapped the ankle in bandages soaked in cold beer for want of water, and I forbade the expert to walk on it for a week, and for good measure I made up a charm which I have had said over bad sprains of my own since then by Germans who didn't know me, and which went:

> Blood to blood,
> Bone to bone,
> Strength to the sinew,
> Skin strong as stone,
> Oak strong as ash,
> Elm at the end,
> Earth over all.

Everybody within earshot wagged their heads and said what a powerful and efficacious charm that must be, and that you hadn't to worry who was going to do the magic as long as you had a Greek about, but ask them to do hard work . . . not likely. Then while Donar was busy helping the patient to a bench, which had to be cleared of novices sitting boasting and rubbing charcoal into their cuts to make them show up better, I slipped out. Me for bed, I thought, if only I can remember which is my hut.

Her warm arm slipped under mine, her warm body pressed to me. Out of the dark she asked:

'Spear-bearer from the South, Greek going north, Joy-knower, Joy-bringer?'

'And if I am?'

There had been no women at the feast. The serving women were not fit to meet the likes of us; nor were the likes of us, strangers, foreigners, of no known clan or lineage, fit to meet Haro's wife or daughters. But this was no serving maid, these hands did not spend the mornings on the quern, grinding out the flour for the day. She smelt sweet, and her voice was gentle not shrill, as she said softly, 'Come, come.'

At that age, that was a call I would never resist. She led me

38

towards a tangle of huts, barns, stables, all mixed together. The tangled clouds raced past the rising moon. The wind caught my hair and hers and mixed them. She pointed up and said:

'You hear the dogs of Wude?'

And indeed the wind sounded faintly, if you wished to think so, like a pack of hunting dogs belling. We came to one hut among many, and she pushed open the unbarred door. The floor was spread with sweet fresh rushes, and the walls hung with embroidered cloths. All round the room were bronze lamps, imported, and probably bought from the family, I thought. They lit her fair skin, her fine face, her long golden hair against my black, as she sank back on the great bed, and spread with furs, furs, a king's ransom in furs, and spread over with silk, an Empress's dowry in fine silk.

I asked her name.

'Gerda,' she told me. The wind howled in the roof.

'Listen,' she cried. 'He rides! The wild hunt rides.'

It was daylight, hardly daylight, the first light. Donar was shaking me, saying:

'Never know where to look for you when you've had a few. Lucky you didn't go for the women, then you would take some finding, bit by bit. Do you know what they do up here?' his voice went maundering on. I looked up at the sky. I lay on a mouldering pile of roof straw in a ruined hut. The door sagged from one leather hinge. Painted plaster peeled damp from the walls. Spring flowers, buds still unopened for the day, sprouted from the turf floor. The wind still howled through the rafters. Where was the huntsman now?

3

We left as soon as it was fairly light. For more days we rode across the uplands, and then through more mountains. Away to the west there rose one great peak that the Germans called the Old Father, the mountain where the world had begun. We left it behind and came down into a country of forests and marshes, and wide rivers.

Then one day about noon we were making along a forest path when there came out of the scrub two horsemen, poor men, in rags, riding on blankets, one red and blue check, the other no particular colour except dirty. They stopped by the side of the path, and watched us as we went by. They were poor. They had no swords, but they carried the long spears of the country, and on their shields the eye of love, or of piety, might make out the shape of a cat. They watched us pass, and we looked them over as we went by, but none of us spoke. Two spears would not fight with three, that was common sense.

That night, and the following night, we set sentries, that is to say we took it in turns to sit by the fire and watch for the Cat King's men, watch the horses grazing hobbled. We had grown soft and lazy, each night we would build us a hut of branches to sleep in, our spears leaning against the door outside at the sentry's back. The second night, Occa was on watch, when he shouted to us to come.

'The horses' he was yelling, 'the horses' – and as we got into the open air we saw that someone had unhobbled them and was driving them away. We all three ran down the slope towards the horses. Then I thought we were fools to go together, and I turned and sure enough there was someone around the hut. I shouted and ran back, and he went off into the wood like a streak.

All he took was my spear. The other two, being spearmen from boyhood, had grabbed theirs to go after the horses, but I had quite forgotten mine, and gone down drawing my sword.

'Easy come, easy go,' I said. Donar was more worried about the impiety.

'It will bring the thief no luck,' he told us, 'to take something hallowed by the God.'

'More to the point,' said Occa, 'there can only be the two of them now, or they'd have attacked. But they must be

40

expecting more, and they've gone for the others while we can't move.'

For we each of us had, in our bags and in the silver sacks, more than a man will willingly carry for more than a few hundred paces, and there was no going to the north on foot. We argued a bit, and the upshot was that we agreed that Occa should go back on foot to find Marcomen of his own clan, and come in a day or two to rescue us. We two would look after the silver.

Occa rubbed wood ash into the pig fat on his face and arms till he was black as night. He left his cloak and wore only his tunic and trousers. He looked for a while at his sword. It was a fine piece of work, made somewhere in the Lebanon, beaten with the cedar charcoal that makes the iron so hard. The hilt was of beech wood carved into the shape of a coiled serpent, and for a pommel he had a great ball of crystal. The scabbard was of soft leather, embossed with the figures of Leda and the Swan, and all tooled with gold leaf, and sewn with gold wire. It was a lovely thing, and it took him long to decide to leave it on his bag, and go off with his spear and his shield and his long hunting knife. He moved away into the forest, silently.

I sat and talked with Donar.

'Why did you come south?' I asked him. It was no use asking him where he had come south from, or what was his nation, he turned all that aside, though there were some who said he talked like a kingless Vandal.

'I came to learn more about sword making,' he said. 'I wanted to know if there was any magic about the swords of the Legions that carried them through Gaul and on to the edge of Germany.'

'And was there?'

'None at all. Rather poor iron, most of it. We make better. Even the way you fight one by one, push and jab, push and jab, all the time, is more comical than anything else. But in a battle, it's the centurion who fights, and the cohort is his weapon.'

We lay and watched for the dawn.

'Talking of centurions,' I said, 'I wonder what Aristarchos is doing now.'

'Getting out of Julia's bed, I shouldn't wonder. You know, he never expected you to get out of the way so smartly when he told you to.'

'What do you mean?'

'He hired these two men to watch you and then told you some cock-and-bull story about Scapellus coming back. He thought if you didn't turn up, he could get straight into bed with Julia, and if you stayed indoors for a couple of days she'd never look at you again. So he told you Scapellus was coming back . . . Funny thing, though . . .'

'What?'

'Old Occa had it from a friend in the Legion headquarters, he wouldn't tell Aristarchos, you know how these legionaries like to spite the cavalry. Scapellus *was* coming back at dawn, after all. I wonder if Aristarchos got up in time. I think it's dawn now. What about breakfast? I think we've got plenty of bacon.'

That day we took it in turns to sit on the kit-bags outside the hut, while turn and turn about we dug a hole in the hut floor, four feet deep, with our knives and our bleeding fingers. There we buried the silver-bags. We stacked our firewood in the hut too. We already had our plan, though we didn't think there would be any need for it for days, if at all. But the other Cat men must have come up sooner than they were expected, because that evening, while Donar was going down to the stream to get some water, they rushed me.

I looked up from where I was sitting, and there they were, a dozen of them, coming at me from the edge of the woods. I knew what to do. I picked a brand from our fire and threw it into the hut, and I shouted:

'Run, Donar, run, hide!' as loudly as I could.

Then one of them came at me with a spear, and I got my sword out, it always would stick and need a tug when I tried it, but that evening it came clean out like a flash. The man with the spear must have met swordsmen before, and when I parried he slipped through my parry, and though he didn't

42

spit me the spear went through my tunic and tore my side. While I was trying not to scream and struggling to get back into the on guard position, someone else must have knocked me on the head. Down I went.

When I knew about things again I just lay still with my eyes shut. After a bit I could open my eyes without moving. That wasn't caution. After you've been knocked out you don't want to do anything but lie still for a long time. And you feel so sick. There was a lot of noise. They were arguing over where the silver had gone. They couldn't look in the hut till the fire died down, and anyway, simple men that they were, they couldn't believe that we'd burn the hut with the silver inside. I could see a pair of puttees and very worn shoes near my face. This man was talking.

'We've only got one of them. If we wait around here too long we'll have Occa and half his clan here after us – '

'We've got his sword,' said somebody.

'Aye, good sword that.'

'The King will want that.'

The first man managed to make himself heard again.

'We'll wake this one up and make him tell us where the silver is.'

'Wake him? Make him? How do you do that?'

'How do you think? A bit of fun that'll be.'

'A bit of fun, and them two listening out there?'

'It'll bring them back.'

'Them, and who else with them? We're not risking that.'

There seemed to be, to say the least, a division of authority in this band.

Someone new put in, the intellectual of the group obviously, with a compromise.

'Take him somewhere else and have your fun there. Don't do it where we can hear it.'

They brought a horse up, and somebody picked me up bodily, grey cloak and all, and slung me across the crupper in front of the rider.

'D'you want his spear?'

'Of course. I stuck him with it, didn't I?'

43

'They say Donar put his name on it. Stands to reason, don't it, if your name's on it, it'll get you.'

'I'll have his bag, too. The brown one, that's what he was carrying.'

The horse laboured under the load. My wound had begun to clot, but heaving me on to the animal's back had opened it again. The horse smelt the blood and jibbed, and the jerking about made the wound hurt more, and my head throbbed. As the pain tightened, I went out again.

I opened my eyes at the pale light of dawn. Everything was pain – my head, my side. I saw life through a mist of pain. Carefully through my pain I felt myself beneath my cloak. I still had my knife, the one that had pointed to Joy. I held my knife in my pain. The horse stopped. He got down. I could not remember who or what had given me pain. I only knew that I must increase pain, breed pain, multiply pain, bring pain to its highest power.

He took me by the shoulders to pull me off.

I stabbed him through the cloak, under the ribs and up. The man screamed, the horse screamed. Through pain I knew where pain lived. We fell together. I was on top. I struck and struck as he screamed, to the groin, to the face I slashed at his eyes, he vomited blood, he jetted blood and pain. The knife had gone, I held hair. Through pain I beat his head on the ground, I felt bone break.

He had been a long time dead. He had been long out of pain. The painful river ran with painful noise. The painful sun was high. Somehow I must see what I was left with.

The horse had gone. He was still there. He had a bag, on the ground near him, with sausage. He had a water bottle, full. I washed my face, swilled out my mouth. A little farther was another water bottle; mine, empty.

I felt I could look at him. The flies crawled in his eyes. I took my knife from his armpit. I cleaned it in the ground, I washed the blood with water. I made myself eat some sausage. I brought it up. I ate more. I must.

I turned him over. He stank. His clothes were tattered. My cloak was bloody, but his was foul, drenched in blood and worse. There was a wallet on his belt. I cut it away; a few silver pieces, a lump of Amber. I knew what I was going to do. I wanted rope. I turned him over and over. Round his waist, not rope, a chain, an iron chain, a gang chain, with places for the necks, and a lock. No key. Where to look for the key?

He had a bronze ring. Why should a man wear a bronze ring? Those keys with a finger ring on the end are common enough here, but I found it hard to think of one there. But even in this wilderness, the chain was Roman, the lock was Roman. The key must be Roman.

Those tales you have heard of cutting off a finger from a body to take a ring. They are true. I did it. I had the key. I put it on my own finger.

I could move a little now. I rolled him fifty paces to the edge of the river. It might have been a mile. We were on the outside of a bend, where the stream ran deep and fast and had cut the bank into a low cliff. I pushed him over into the water. He floated away. I never knew his name.

I lowered the water bottles by their straps and filled them. I soaked the shirt away from my wound. It was long and ragged but not deep. If I could lie up somewhere for a few days I might be fit enough to walk back to Haro's farm. Cat men could follow the trail we had left, wolves could smell the blood. I must move on.

I reckoned that I could make perhaps a mile in the hour. It was slower going than that. After a few steps I stepped on my spear lying in the long grass, where it had fallen. I used it as a staff. It was easier then. I moved away from the river, through the scrub, alder and willow. I went up hill. There was nothing to my purpose. I had the set mind of the mad. No sane man would have done what I did.

I came out of the scrub. There was about half a mile of open space before the edge of the forest itself. There were charred stumps, spongy earth. The clearing had been burnt, frequently. No trees, nothing but grass had grown over it. In the centre of the clearing, too old and huge for a grass fire to harm, was an oak tree.

45

The oak in the burnt land should have warned. The scraps of rag and fur in the branches, the broken jars at the foot, the horse skulls around, should have told what it was. I was mad. Wolves could not climb a tree. Cat men could not see through a curtain of fresh leaves. Who sent me mad?

I got into the crown of the tree, a man's height above the ground. Too high for wolves to jump? Every movement now tore at my knitting side, my brains flowed loose in my skull. I leant against a limb. The chain I passed round my body and the branch, and I locked it. The ring was on my finger. If I could wake three days on the heaving deck pressing down on the steering oar, then I could sleep three days in the still tree.

The light was going. The chain hurt. My head ached, my side burnt. It was bitterly cold. It was dark, darker than night, darker than a cave, darker than death.

4

That night the Most Holy One, the God himself, came to me. There are many appearances of Apollo, and you who have been brought up here in Rome know only Apollo the Youth, the Singer. But you who have never been to the Old City cannot know the God as He stands there in the Sanctuary. The God came from the Islands long ago and chose his own Temple. The God, the Father of Aesculapius, is an old man, long-haired, long-bearded, as indeed I was in those days. He is the Healer and the Destroyer, Apollo Paeon.

He stood before me in the tree, in breech clout and scarlet cloak, as he stands in the Sanctuary. All the night long he stood before me as He so long stood before our Fathers. For He is our Father, we are His sons, and before His son the Father stood the night through.

Near dawn I asked Him:

'Father Paeon, why are you here? Why are we here?'

He answered, 'When you stood with Joy at the river bank, when you took Joy's spear in your hand, did you not vow to go where I should send you? Now shall you pay your vow, and see the Hyperboreans from whence I came.'

'And what shall I do there, my Father?'

'Is not my name Apollo, and does it not mean Destruction? You shall bring destruction to all who are safe and contented. In the shadow of light shall you bring them the darkness of fire.'

Apollo brought the dawn as I hung in my chain. I moistened my lips as the sun came up, and I wished I could risk eating again, but the sausage was salty and my water would last three days at the most with great care. Toward noon, Apollo sent a sign. The cloud came over and there was a thunderstorm. My clothes were soaked, I drank the water that poured through my hair. I licked the water from the leaves and I ate. There was a hollow in the tree just in front of me that filled with water and I could just reach it, straining against the chain.

If I let the chain out, if I unlocked it and let it out a link or two, I would still be safe, I could reach the water without rasping the wound, I would – I had no key. There was no key on my finger, or in the wallet. Not on the ground beneath. There it was, a foot beyond my reach, below my reach. It hung on a twig as on a finger. And I could not reach it.

I wriggled and I squirmed. I could not get down to it. I tried to work the chain down, but it wouldn't come, it was stuck on some snag behind the limb. I could not reach round to it. I fought and writhed, and every movement tore at my side, opened the knitting wound, let the blood trickle again down my side. I hung in my chain and looked down. In my agony Apollo had sent a sign. In the grass the hyacinths bloomed as once they bloomed for Amyclos, son of the hyacinth, killed in far Sparta by the disc of Apollo.

As night fell, the God came again, but not as a man. Apollo Lykanthropos came, great grey shadowy forms in the dusk. If you ever come to the Old City and stand in the Sanctuary before the God, you will know what the wolf means to our family.

47

There were a score of them, and that in the late spring, when they hunt singly. They came and went in the dark. Just before dawn, at the time when Apollo spoke to me, when I was almost asleep in spite of my fear and pain and fatigue, the first one leapt. His teeth tore the toe of my shoe. I pulled up my feet into the crown, but still they leapt, not singly, but two or three at a time snapping and slavering. I could smell them, I could feel their spittle on my legs. For an hour in the twilight, the wolves danced, and to my wrist was still tied the spear which I must not use.

Apollo brought the sun, and there were no wolves. I licked the dew from the leaves. There were no clouds. I struggled with the chain, and brought blood. I could not reach the key. When the sun was high, I risked a pull at the water bottle. It was then that I saw the men. They stood at the edge of the wood, and they danced in my eyes so that I could not count them. I tried to shout, but I had no voice. They were not there any more.

Then it was dark again, and light again. I do not know how often the dark and the light came. Or how often the wolves danced. After a while there was no water in the bottles. Only the dew and sometimes the rain. And the pain. I hung forward on the chain in pain. My head was an expanding flame, my mouth a sea of dust. And there was hunger, the worst hunger of all, for I had food that I dare not touch, the salt sausage.

There were creatures in the tree that crawled on the leaves, the slimy and hairy and creeping things that no man may eat. Yet I think that I tried to eat, and then I think I retched. There were squirrels and birds, yet not one that came within reach of my spear. Somewhere in the tree were bees. And there was something in the tree I never saw, though I heard him slither in the branches and once I felt his long body trail across my thighs. Yet he was a comfort, how should any snake, python or not, harm a man vowed to Apollo?

The wolves danced, and the rain drove through my cloak, and the sun glared down on the empty land. And I saw. How far can you see from six feet up in an oak tree, on the edge of a forest in the plain? I tell you, I saw from sea to sea and from beginning to end. And the ghosts of the dead may haunt you, and the dread of them bring you to madness; but the ghosts of them who are doomed yet to be born – I tell you what I know, I tell you nothing that I have not seen, and the dread of that is too much for any mortal man. Look at my hair and know how dread it was.

In the east there is nothing. Nothing at all. There are more men than ever you could dream of. But every man looks exactly like his neighbour, and every generation is exactly like every other generation. Nor is there ever any change or ever anything new.

But to the west, the whole land is a pot of porridge and the walls of the Empire are the sides of the pot. Every bubble in the porridge is a nation and nations are born as the bubbles burst. In the end the pot will boil over. For it is not the pot only that boils over but the very air.

I told you that in those days it was warmer than it is now, and you thought that it was the delusion of an old man trying to keep his bones from freezing.

But I know that Apollo himself comes and goes as he pleases, and that sometimes he withdraws the Chariot of the Sun from the earth, and sometimes comes nearer, and between the warmest and the coldest times may be hundreds of years.

From six feet up in the oak tree, while the snake moved about me and above me and behind me, I saw the cold and the heat come and go, age on age, from the tree to the ocean, and beyond the ocean. For there are lands beyond the ocean. As I hung in my chains, Apollo let me see in my pain that he is even now withdrawing from the earth. As the earth got colder, the porridge boiled over and swamped into the Empire. And as porridge which boils over is burnt and charred and changed into ash, so the barbarians who will boil over into the Empire will be changed and transmuted and charred into new nations, neither Roman nor Barbarian. And every one of these nations that is changed will be led by the sons of Votan, who lead only because they are Votan-born. And the Votan-born will spread over the whole earth, and whatever people they conquer they will turn into something like themselves.

The colder it gets, and the farther Apollo goes from the earth, the more the nations of the Votan-born will turn to the sea, and go out to face the storms of the ocean, and the terrors that lie beyond the ocean. But when Apollo approaches nearer the earth, then they will turn to the east. And in the east they will have little luck. They will conquer no land, nor will they change any nation, but rather will they be changed themselves.

My tree, the oak tree, stood somewhere in the borders between east and west. Beneath it I saw the Votan-born lead their people against the east, and the east ride back over their bodies. And when they had any success and ruled for a time over the east, the east in time always swallowed them up.

Yet the Votan-born ride against the east again and again. Sometimes they ride in the name of an Emperor who was a God, and sometimes in the name of an Emperor who knew no God, and sometimes in the name of a God who could not be an Emperor, because he was a God of Peace, and sometimes they ride in the names of no one but themselves. But whether they ride cased in furs against the cold or cased in iron against the arrows, whether they fight with swords or with fire, they ride against the east because the east rides against them. And always they die. Some die well, in battle or in bed. Some die ill, of dysentery or plague, or drowned in a ditch or crammed in a barn and burnt. And near the end of time, they will die not well or badly, but miserably, passionlessly, wretchedly, hopelessly, walking in naked columns to choke.

And at the end of time – there will be an end of time. After the Votan-born have made the greatest of music, and have painted the greatest of pictures and sung the greatest songs that can ever be, then the east will come against them for the last time. And then, knowing clearly what they do, but not knowing whose will they do, the Votan-born will dissolve the whole world in fire, and they will return to the Sun whose sons they are.

Out of that glare of fire I woke to the glare of noon. The men came, and I could not speak to them. They came to the very foot of the tree, and before my dry eyes they poured out cool, clear, bitter beer at the roots. Then they too were gone.

After that my head became very heavy. I saw every thing far away yet very clear as when you look through glass into clear water, at shells and little fishes. I knew I was going to die. I watched the empty land and watched myself die.

At sunset there was a thunderstorm, and the rain ran into the hollow, and I drank. Then I slept till I woke in the darkness. There was someone in the tree. You must know that there cannot be Apollo without Artemis. You cannot love the wolf and hate the bear. I heard her scramble into the branches, and the little twigs break beneath her. I heard her claws scratch on the bark. Then the bear turned to me, hairy chest against my chest, face against my face, breath mixed with my breath, cold teeth smooth against my cheek. She stayed while I might count a hundred. Then she climbed up, and I knew by the sounds that she had found the bees' nest. Honey, wild honey, poured down on to my head and face, and I licked it off. The wolves did not come.

Toward dawn, the God stood before me again, and spoke.

'Go north, and begin the End for me. But do not call upon my name till you come again within the cities of the Empire. For long ago I left the Hyperboreans. Where you find peace, you will leave war, and where stability, confusion, and where trust, deceit. But all in all you shall do my will.'

Then I felt that the snag at the back of the limb was broken, and the chain ran smoothly up and down the tree. I saw myself alone and wounded and hungry on the great plain, and I thought that it no longer mattered.

I was very far gone. The whole world seemed far away. I stood back and looked at myself. I saw how slow I was in thinking and I marvelled at it. I saw that my limbs trembled like an old man's. I watched my own mind work slowly through the argument that if my chain was slack I ought to be able to reach the key. After an hour or more, I saw myself decide to try. Very slowly I worked the chain down the tree. For some reason I was afraid that I might fall.

Little pieces fell out of my time of life, little holes of blackness. My side was a dull glow that fanned into flame every time I moved. There was still some water in the hollow. When I had reached the bottom of the chain's movement, I allowed myself a mouthful.

I touched the key once or twice. I hardly believed it was still there. I put the ring on my finger. I opened the lock. The chain fell away. I let my spear fall after it. I finished the water in the hollow; now I could walk, crawl, to more. I slid to the ground, my feet touched the earth; then my face.

When the blackness was over again, I found my spear and leaned it against the tree. I climbed up it, to my knees, to my feet. The men were there, a dozen of them, big men, with shaven heads and long yellow moustaches, dressed in the German fashion but unbelievably shabby. I waited to be killed.

They stood about ten yards from me. They had no weapons at all. One of them, the oldest, I thought, came forward and said something. I could not understand a word. I said in German:

'Drink . . . drink . . .'

One of them, a boy, brought forward a pot. There is nothing like bitter beer for quenching your thirst. I drained it.

The older man then said something in German, very thickly accented. At first I thought he was talking about the Old Father Mountain, and I said 'Yes, Yes' and pointed. He talked on, and I slowly began to follow. He was calling me Old Father — no, he was calling me Allfather. This was wrong. This was what they called the God in Germany. I said: 'No, no, Photinus, I am Photinus,' and the man said,

'Yes, yes, Votan, Votan Allfather. Come, Allfather, come and eat.'

I was too ill to protest any further. I tried to step forward, but I could not move. Some of the men ran back to the edge of the wood, and returned with a litter made of boughs. They helped me on to it, and carried me away. One of the boys carried my spear erect before me. Another picked up my bag, turned it inside out, and under the horrified gaze of his seniors gobbled up the end of sausage left in it. Before the older men, crimson with rage and shame, could begin to scold, I said, 'Eat, eat it all!'

Another man picked up my two water bottles and shook them. There was a swishing sound. One of them still had about a pint of water. Had I, in my delirium, always gone to the same bottle to drink, and always found it empty?

They carried me some miles along the river edge to where they lived in little huts of boughs. They were a wandering people with neither king nor cities nor any possessions, not even any iron, who lived on what they could gather and catch along the river and in the woods. For their clothes and pots, and even for corn, they traded the furs they caught through the winter.

'We take them,' said the headman, who said his name was Tawalz, 'to the Asers, and they give us the good things of life.'

'Who are the Asers?' I asked him, for this was a name I had not heard before. But all Tawalz would say was, 'We take you to Asers, you meet Asers, first you heal.'

In one of the huts, Tawalz and some old women cut and soaked away the shirt from my wound, and — and this shows how poor they were — one of the old women took my shirt away and carefully darned up the tears, and washed it and brought it back to me. First they cared for the scabby weals the chain had made on my chest, and the scratches from the branches and the insect bites. They brought ointment

53

to smear on, but I would not let them use it till I was sure that it was not bear fat.

Over the great festering wound in my side they were more concerned. Tawalz said:

'It is not deep but it will remain open till we can find the healing stone that is upon the sword and lay it upon the wound.'

'It was no sword,' I said. 'It was a spear, and my own spear, that the lad carried into camp.'

So they brought the spear, and just like any civilised doctor Tawalz put ointment on the head and bound it up and vowed the hurt of the wound to the God, and then cleaned the wound itself and bandaged it.

I wanted to sleep, but the old women, all anxious, said through Tawalz that I must eat first. They brought me stewed meat in a bowl, and when I tasted it, it was something that I had not tasted for years, it was horse. I asked them why horse, and Tawalz said:

'Allfather, it is a horse for you.'

They had caught a horse loose in the forest, and while you or I, if we found a stray horse, and there was no danger of being caught, would use it or sell it, they knew no better than to take it to the tree, which was all the temple that they had, and sacrifice it. But to my horror, it became clear that the horse was sacrificed to me, and now they expected me to eat it all. Have you ever tried to eat a whole horse? The old ladies were very insistent that I should. First I could eat it fresh, and then I would have it salt, and with the offal and the intestines they could make sausages, and they were busy cleaning the skin to make a blanket for my bed. I forget what they were going to do with the hooves.

I managed to get over to them the idea that if the sacrifice were to me, then I could do as I liked with it. So I would give a feast to the whole clan. And since it is no use eating flesh alone, I gave some of the silver pieces from the wallet for two of the young men to run twelve hours each way to the nearest German farm, where they had an arrangement, to buy corn, salt and beer. Then they let me sleep.

But before I slept I looked at my hair as it lay on the pillow, and I grew afraid. I asked for a mirror, and of course they had no such thing, but when they understood at last they brought me a bowl of water. When it was still I looked at my reflection in the water. My face was lined and haggard, as I expected. What I did not expect was this, that in those days on the tree, my hair and my beard had changed from black to white. From that day to this, I have been as you see me, a white-haired man, and for years I bore an old man's head on a young man's body. It is not at all a bad thing in many ways. It gives you an authority, a reputation which you would not otherwise possess, and old men and chieftains bow to you and call you Father, or even Allfather. White-haired Photinus I have been ever since, and it was as a white-haired man that I came to the Northern Sea and faced the Asers.

6

I slept for twenty-four hours, as far as I could guess. When I woke, they brought me my clothes, all washed and pressed with smooth stones, and they also brought me all the horse furniture. This was not only the rope harness and iron bit and a few iron fittings, but the blanket too, red and blue check, and my own kit-bag. So I went to their feast in all dignity in my best blue tunic, and I drank from my own silver cup, and I ate off my own silver plate. We ate the horse; forty of us left little of a horse, or of a couple of deer and a few dozen carp with it. There was enough beer for all the adults to drink their fill, and even for the children to taste. The women, as well as the men, sat round the fire to eat.

These people are used to eating but once a day, and that not every day. Their bread was the worst I tasted in the north, being over half acorn and birch pith mixed with the flour. They called themselves the Polyani, from their word for the river meadows in which they lived; and they were proudly distinct from the Rus, who spoke the same language and lived in the same way, but farther east on the wide plains of grass, next to the yellow men, or the Lesny, who lived in the forests between.

I tried to find out who or what they thought I was.

'Joy led us to Allfather, joy told us he was here,' said Tawalz, and I was never sure if I had understood him correctly. 'We come to the tree, and we see Allfather chained there to hunger and to thirst. Yet there is water in his bottles, and there is food in his bag. We see the wolf dance to Allfather, and we see the bear come to feed Allfather and bring him honey. And at the end we see Allfather bend down for his magic and unlock his chain and step from the tree.'

'How many days was I in the tree?' I asked.

'Oh, many days, many days,' said Tawalz. 'Many days – nine days.' But later I realised that nine was an indefinite number to them, more than several and less than many. I was never sure how they regarded me, as the epiphany of a God or as a Holy Man fulfilling a vow. We talked of other things. I told them of cities. They listened, and then said:

'Oh, yes, like Asgard.'

'What is Asgard?' I asked, but they had never been there, they only knew it was where the Asers, most of them, lived, and if it were not a city then it was recognisably like one. I talked about Egypt, and I told them of the elephant. They said, yes, they knew all about elephants, and they drew one in the sand to show that they knew exactly what I meant. They said that far to the north of them was a desert, but a desert of ice, not of sand, and this is reasonable, for the earth is perfect and symmetrical and there must be deserts of cold to balance the deserts of heat. In those deserts too, it seems, there live elephants, but they do not wander about the earth. There they burrow underground, seeking in the heart of the earth the warmth they cannot find on the surface. When they come to the surface the light kills them at once, and so they are often found at the end of the winter, which is one long night, dead half-way out of their burrows in the ground. The Polyani and the Rus call them Mamunt.

The Polyani had no real Gods, only a few spirits of pools and woods and rivers, that were better bribed than worshipped. Where they felt the need, they borrowed the Gods of the richer people around, the Germans, or farther east, the Scyths, or in the south the Greeks. Tawalz said:

'We knew you would come, Allfather, because long ago, in Grandfather's Grandfather's time, a man came talking about a God, who hung on a tree, and was wounded with a spear. He said this God would come to us alive. We do not know it is Allfather.'

I asked who this man was, but they could not tell me, except that he would not eat wild boar. At the end, they had been forced to do what he seemed, to the best of their understanding, to be asking them to do. They ate him and drank his blood. This had been a most repugnant thing for Tawalz's ancestors, and only their excess of courtesy, and their desire to do whatever their guest requested, had brought them to do it. Besides, the tradition was that he tasted vile, and most of him had been decently burnt. They hoped that this minor waste did not offend me. This was the only thing they told me that I found it difficult to believe.

It took another ten days or so after the feast before my side was healed well enough to travel. I was very weak, and I spent the time sitting at the river bank fishing. There are no Votan-born among the Polyani. I watched Tawalz and his brother Olen build the raft on which they would take the winter's catch of furs, bundled up by kind, down river to, they said, Outgard, wherever that might be, to sell, they said, to Loki, whoever he might be.

'Is he an Aser?' I asked, and they hummed and hawed, and were of two minds.

'Is he an Amber King?' I asked, and of that too they were uncertain. They only knew that he was the man who would sell them iron and cloth and salt for their furs. They had very little iron. There was but the one axe in the whole band, and that among people who lived on the forest edge. The raft they built well, of logs jointed and dowelled together, with a little shelter, for us to sleep in.

In the end we went off, Tawalz and Olen and I. There was little poling to do, the river carried us on, and we would stop for the night near the camps of other little bands of Polyani. I could not follow much that they said, but I knew that the tale of the white-haired man who starved on purpose wounded in a tree, attended by wolves and snakes, was travelling well ahead of us. The further we got, the greater the respect with which I was treated, and of course some of this consideration rubbed off on to Tawalz. Later it profited him.

7

One afternoon we came to Outgard. The river was wide and shallow, fordable for a man on foot. We grounded the raft on a sloping beach on the east side of the stream. The two Polyani humped the bales of furs out on to the bank. Tawalz led me up from the water's edge to the beginning of a path paved with logs. At the end of the path well above the flood level was the long black line of a palisade. Olen came behind. I looked back at the bales of furs, abandoned.

'Will they be safe?' I asked.

'Of course,' said Tawalz. 'Look, here come porters. And up there, see? Vandals.'

There were three or four Germans lounging at the gates, different from the crowd of Polyani who passed us as they went to carry the furs in. The men at the gate were big men in all their gear, with spears, shields, and, something I had not seen before in the north, mail shirts. They wore helmets, second-hand legionary pattern, and each had a blue cloak. I found out later that this was a batch of cloth that Loki had bought as a speculation and been unable to sell, so he had paid his Vandals in cloth.

'Loki keeps them here. Nobody steals furs. Loki sits within the gate.'

And he did. By all the rules, looking back, I should have hated Loki. In fact I rather liked him. I kept on liking him, really, right up to the end. He was young then, about thirty, and my build, fair hair and blue eyes, of course. He was the first German I ever met who was a dandy. He was wearing a red shirt and blue trousers, and yellow puttees matching his yellow cloak. He had soft leather knee boots and a soft leather belt, two palms wide, worked with a pattern of silver wire. Round his neck hung a great globe of Amber on a golden chain.

He carried no sword, and I tell you, he was clean. He wasn't as clean, say, as an auxiliary trooper going on duty, but he was about as clean as the Polyani who spend all their time in and out of the water. The Polyani, though, never bothered to brush the mud off. Loki was a great deal cleaner than the Marcomen.

Loki was more like a Greek than any German I ever met. Not, of course, like one of those stupid dolts from Attica or the Peloponnese, but like one of your bright lads from Rhodes or Alexandria. He was a merchant, and there he sat at the gate in a kind of booth, with his scales and his measures on the table. He spoke to Tawalz, as soon as we appeared, in the good old beat-'em-down-below-cost manner.

'What do you think you're doing here? Far too late, far too late.'

Tawalz was used to this. He said,

'Furs. Fine furs, you never saw better. Such you never see again.'

'It's been a bad year, all down the river. Poor stuff, take it away.'

'No, all good fur, first rate. It surprised us all. *He* brought it.'

'Who's "he"?'

I had been standing carefully withdrawn from the scene. With my old grey cloak pulled around me, I leaned on my spear and looked round, inside the palisade. It was a big enclosure, a hundred and fifty paces each way, and all as neat and tidy as a legionary fort. At my right, along one side, was a double row of barns and stables. At the other side were huts, obviously for people. In front of me, at the far side, was a great hall, twice as big as Haro's, with a huddle of kitchens and larders behind. In the open space in front was a kind of market with stalls, and a great throng of men buying and selling.

But Outgard was not a city. In the first place, there were no women, and certainly no confused crowd of children who got under your feet in the smallest German village. Secondly, that palisade was no wall, but a frail fence, built to keep horses in, not thieves out. Like all the houses, the fence had a temporary look. Even the fresh coat of tar merely made it look newer, less rooted. But it was something to look at while I withdrew my gaze from Tawalz who was whispering to Loki about 'Nine days . . . wolves . . . bear . . .honey.' Then Loki called out,

'Hey, you! Greybeard!'

I just didn't hear him, till he used my name and asked, 'Votan! Where do you come from, and where are you going?'

So I paid him for his calculated discourtesy with a long stare, and then:

'If I fight with Mamunt below the earth, or ride the sky beyond the clouds, what is it to you where I go?' And to illustrate, I swung my spear point in a great arc from ground to sky to ground, and everyone watched the shining arc, and nobody saw my hands at all.

Loki didn't try to answer that, he just wanted time to think, now that the rumours he had heard had come true. So he returned,

'No gossiping in business hours. Eat at my right hand tonight. There will be a hut for you, for you alone. Tawalz will show you.'

I turned away, but Loki hadn't finished.

'Hey, that spear. No one goes armed in Outgard. Leave it with the Vandals at the gate!'

There was no harm in leaving him the appearance of authority. I leaned over his table and stood the spear in the corner of his booth, behind his back.

'Take care of it,' I said. 'A God gave it to me. The last man who touched it without leave is dead.'

Off I went toward the market. Nobody who tries to sound as businesslike as that should be allowed an inch of latitude. Five paces from the booth, I turned and called to Loki.

'Keep your eyes on the stock, merchant! Catch!' And I threw him the Amber globe.

8

Now how was I to dine with the Lord of the Amber Road in my rags? I had only two or three silver coins, and my silver cup and plate which I would need. It was like taking a cake from a blind baby. Those poor Germans never knew what hit them.

The first group I came to were playing the old game with three cups and a pea. Now I will not ask you to believe that I invented it; but Autolycus did, and he was staying with the Family at the time. I watched a bit, and gossiped.

'Come far?'

'Thuringia. Back tomorrow, thank heaven.'

I lost a diplomatic denarius.

'What did you bring up?'

'Usual. Linen out, back in furs. Ferdi there, he came up in glass. Risky trade that, but profitable.'

'Any Amber?'

'Not here, you'll have to go to Asgard for it. Loki buys it in from the forest dwellers, and the furs, but he only sells furs. The Amber all goes back to Asgard, and Njord only sells for silver.'

I put the rest of my silver down. The dealer covered it and I took him. In another four passes I cleaned him out. Then I took the cups and won what the rest of the school had between them. Then I allowed everybody to win something back, and even let the dealer have enough to start again, so I went off letting them all think that the game had been fair.

The next pair were playing the finger game. You know, I shoot out fingers and you shout a number at the same time. If you are right, you win. This sounds like pure chance, but you watch people playing. They think they are shouting at random, but everyone has favourite numbers, and if you watch a man for a little you can always work out his system. Then you can take him as far as you like. I did. I didn't clean them out, just took enough to do the job.

What they lost was mostly silver jewellery, and a very few coins. I went to one of the market stalls. There was a Vandal behind it. All the stalls belonged to Loki. There were Vandals behind them all. I got a grey tunic, grey trousers, good boots, a soft belt. Then something caught my fancy, and I bought a big grey hat with a floppy brim. I asked about a cloak as long as the one I had on, and I was promised delivery next morning. They were fairly popular, the man said, but not in grey, the colour wasn't really worth stocking. No German will wear grey, or that dark blue the Vandals used, if he can possibly help it.

I thought of the two Polyani. I had given Olen my blue tunic because he hadn't got one at all, but his trousers were all right. I got a suit for Tawalz, nothing fancy, but tough, and boots for the pair of them. Then I added a few iron fish hooks and a dozen iron arrow points. You know, they were used to going in after boar with bone-tipped arrows, and they hadn't got the penetration to slow the beast up at all.

Then I was down to my last few silver pieces again. But at least I was respectable. With three silver pieces I could start again. I had a set of loaded dice in my bag. There were two or three likely prospects I'd marked down. There was even one who might go for a gold brick – or would it be a silver one up here? That could wait till an emergency. Did I tell you, once in Alexandria I sold the Pharos to three different people in one day, and another day, the whole Library?

9

So, decent, we went into the hall. And though they firmly settled Olen near the door, the Vandals put Tawalz fairly well up, and me, of course, they led to sit with Loki at the top table.

No, Loki told me, he wasn't a Vandal. He seemed pleased to talk to me, to have somebody new to talk to must have been rare. He said he was an Aser.

'Yes, I came out here some years ago, and I took Outgard over completely when my uncle Bergelmir . . . left. It's a bit lonely, but quite comfortable.'

Loki was comfortable. On the top table we had silver-mounted drinking horns, and silver plate. And we had wine to drink, only Italian of course, but still better than beer. I was telling Loki how much better the wine would be with a lacing of sea-water, when a big man, rather drunk, but not so drunk he wasn't nasty, stood in front of us and threw down his cloak on the floor. That, I knew, was a challenge to fight any man in the house. I tried to ignore it, but he didn't ignore me. There were no takers – the man on my right whispered that Grude was a notorious bully – so he leant on the top table and taunted me with cowardice, age, and stupidity. None of which was true. I don't like to say that Loki had arranged this, but there would have been no fight in his hall without his approval, and it was an attractive chance of getting rid of two nuisances at once.

Grude leant over and leaned his elbows on the table and breathed beer all over me with a stream of insults that would have withered the whiskers off a boar. When I sat there like a log, Loki helped by sneering:

'You'll be all right, I'll lend you a mail shirt.'

Of course, I was fool enough to say, 'I have no sword,' and at once there was a Vandal at my elbow with a whole bundle of them which their owners had deposited with him at the door for safe keeping. He offered me the hilts, and I shut my eyes and took one at random.

The God guided my hand. There was a roar of laughter in the hall, and Grude snatched the weapon away from me. It was his own sword. For a moment he looked as if he were going to throw it away, but then he must have felt a bit sheepish and he kept it. Still, it unsettled him for the evening, and I think it was really the death of him.

I turned my head away again, and took another, and again the God guided me. This was no German sword, I thought, this was a Greek Kopis like my own, not too long, pointed, one edge sharp, the other finger-thick, the bone breaker.

I had heard that they had been once in fashion all over Germany. Now they only lingered in the far west.

This I could use. The weight of the blade was a little far forward for my liking, but otherwise the balance was perfect. I passed it from hand to hand, tossed it up and caught it, and tried a few wrist flicks. It was then that some people began to realise that this was a real contest, and I heard the odds shorten. I looked around to get a few denarii on before it came down to evens, but somebody got in the way, holding out an oilstone and saying,

'Make her sharp, make my little Jutta sharp.' He was a middle-aged man with a thick north-western accent. 'Treat her well, she is thirsty, my sax.'

It was obvious that he was a little afraid of having the costly blade damaged.

'She'll be all right,' I told him. 'I shed no blood.'

He caught my eye and my meaning. With the look of one craftsman meeting another, he held the sword up and breathed on the blade, below the hilt.

'Look, a snake sword,' and, sure enough, in the torchlight little snakes twisted in the iron.

I held Jutta comfortably and stood on a stain at one corner of the cloak. I kept my back to Loki; I didn't want those eyes on mine. Someone gave me a shield, and I threw it away. This gave Grude first stroke, although he was the challenger, but it forced him to throw away his shield too. He wasn't used to fighting like that, but I was, and what use are rules if you can't use them?

I had to think of tactics. I couldn't try to tire him out, I was still weak from the tree. I didn't want to go moving around over the mutton bones. I knew what to do, but a lot of people were shouting advice, and examples of excellent wit like, 'Show him your stuffing, Votan.' Nobody seemed to be shouting for Grude, and it was just as well, the whole thing didn't last long.

We took guard, Loki shouted, 'Ready!', and Grude tried a downward cut. He was a bit clumsy, and I just pushed his sword away and instead of cutting myself I carried the

64

parry on into a jab-jab-jab at his eyes. I thought I might force him off the cloak; but he'd met this before, and now he tried a cut, roundarm, almost horizontal. So nothing was easier than to counter by bringing the blunt edge of Jutta down on to his wrist, so that we heard the bone crack. The sword went flying and I followed through with all my might on to his kneecap.

He went down like a log, and lay there screaming, which drew some comment, but you will admit that a broken wrist and a smashed kneecap together are rather painful. And then I found out the kind of people I was living with.

A couple of Vandals picked Grude up.

'How is he?' asked Loki.

'His wrist is smashed, and he'll never walk straight again.'

'What use is that to us?' Loki said, and they heaved him up over a bench and somebody cut off his head with his own sword. I believe Loki got hold of his farm after that. They carted out the body and threw sawdust on the floor to stop the dogs licking the blood.

They brought me Grude's belongings, as was right. There was quite a lot of silver coin and a few pieces of gold in a wallet, some scraps of Amber, a gold neck chain, and a gold ring with a big yellow stone in it. Next day, I took Cutha, who owned Jutta, to a goldsmith and he opened the ring and closed it again tightly around the grip, so that shapely sword at last had some adornment. I recited twenty lines of Homer over it, Hector's speech to Andromache which seemed appropriate, and scratched my name in the soft gold, so that Cutha thought Jutta had a real healing stone at last.

But that night, most of the western Germans crowded around me, laughing and shouting congratulations, and so did some of the Vandals. Some of the others said I had not acted fairly in going straight from a parry into a stroke without waiting, but nobody now dared say it close enough for me to hear.

They brought me Grude's sword and shield. I said I didn't want them, though I did keep the belt, which was better than the one I had bought. When I pushed Grude's sword away, Cutha offered me Jutta in exchange, saying, 'She likes you, she'll go with you,' but he was quite drunk, so I said I would have no sword till Donar made me one. At this, some of the Vandals laughed, as if Donar, some Donar, was dead and done for, but the westerners looked very impressed.

In the end I gave Grude's sword, and the shield, to Tawalz. He was the first of all the Polyani to bear arms like a free man, and the first to make his authority felt over more than one band. Trouble and blood came of that gift and little else.

The chain and the silver I used to buy more gifts for the Polyani, spear heads and axes and iron pots, and bolts of linen and woollen cloth. No pottery or glass, which they would dearly have loved, since there was little chance of their getting all the way back unbroken; but I did send bronze brooches for the old ladies who had nursed me, and a bronze mirror that they might see what one looked like.

The return for the furs Tawalz took in grain and beer. This was little in comparison to the furs, and he decided to leave the rest till later in the year. Loki not only did not allow him interest on this debt, but even charged him a fee for storage. He would have done well in Alexandria.

I gave the belt I'd bought to Tawalz. So I had little gain from the bloody affair, indeed I lost, for no one now would fight with me, and there was no chance of persuading anyone that I was qualified to sell him the Amber mines, or wherever they got the stuff. (I never did find out how you get it, and I think someone must have had a fine time telling Tacitus that tale about picking it up on the sea shore.) So it was as a dangerous man and a well-known one that I left Outgard. And through the Vandals and their wives who lived in the village over the ridge, and through the traders who were there that night, all Germany soon knew of the white-haired man from the tree who had come out of the forest.

10

I had two nights at Outgard. The second evening was quiet,

perhaps because I spent most of the day leaning on my spear in front of Loki's booth, and just looking at him as he worked. This unsettled him so much that, in plain language, he offered me a horse to go away to Asgard and annoy somebody else. So I went.

I went in company with the Saxons who had been at the first dinner. They had a packtrain, and a packmaster, a big man with one hand; he had lost his right hand, and carried his shield on his forearm, and his spear in his left. They had been waiting for him to arrive; he came in the day after the fight. As we went the Saxons told me about the Asers. They appeared not sure whether to expect from me omniscience or universal ignorance.

I found out a lot that would have been useful to Otho. The Asers were the lords of the Amber roads. The Polyani lived beyond the river. Beyond them, and to the north-east lived the Scrawlings. North again, across the shallow seas, lived the Goths, who were Germans. It was these peoples who brought in the furs and the Amber. They would only trade with the Asers. The Asers held immense stocks of all they wanted, close to the river and the sea, so that we, if we tried, could never outbid the Asers. All trade had to be through the Asers.

On the other hand, to the traders the Asers supplied packtrains and escorts at low prices, and on the roads between the three great Aser posts, at Outgard, Asgard and Westgard toward the Rhine, they had stopping places for the packtrains.

At one of these we stopped the first night. We rode into a palisade, and there were men to take the horses and stable them, and Vandals to check every bale and put it into the stores. We went into a hall, and we stood in line to receive great platters of stewed meat and vegetables, and bread, and each man his horn of beer. There was as much food as you could eat, as often as you returned for more, but extra beer you had to buy at a counter in the corner. I sat with Cutha and asked, 'Is Loki an Aser?'

'Some say he is, and some say he isn't. He came from Asgard, sure enough, and Njord sent him. And it wasn't long before he drove out Bergelmir, the old man, now he really was an Aser. Where Bergelmir went no one knows, but he strode away vowing vengeance on Njord and Loki and all the Aser house. But Tyr, there, the packtrain leader, now he is an Aser. Look, he's going to tell one of his tales; up on the table, there he goes.'

And up Tyr stood indeed, to give what was always a popular piece, though this was the first time of many that I ever heard it. He had a sausage in his hand, and as he recited he alternately took bites and made obscene gestures.

'It fell, a couple of years ago, at the end of a long wet summer, that Ulla and Hermod and I went to forage down in Thuringia. The pickings weren't very good, not enough to live through the winter, just a few furs and some girls, that we sold off cheap to the Marcomen. All those goods that went straight down, to Carnuntum and Vindabonum, they sold for silver and glass and wine, and all we got was some sausage.'

'What, sausage?' shouted the audience, they weren't subtle and this was the traditional response to Tyr.

'Yes, sausage,' and the one he had was as long as your arm and as thick as your wrist.

'Well, the girls weren't up to much, and we very soon finished the sausage. We hadn't as much as a roof to our heads, when the leaves were beginning to fall. My trousers were full of enormous holes, and Ulla was hardly decent, so Hermod, who was respectable then, said we ought to go on into Dacia. There we'd meet no one who knew us before, and bring no disgrace to our families. At worst we'd beg bread from the peasants and slaves, and we might find a chieftain to feast us.'

'But the people of Dacia are crafty and mean, the crows starve to death in their cornfields. The rags of my bottom were beating my brains out, and the cold struck chill to my liver . . .'

'To your liver?' and they all cheered.

'To my liver. For a good square meal, I'd have gone past the river to ride for a soldier in Britain. It was then that

68

Hermod found us a horse, a fine black horse with a saddle. The man who rode it was drunk in a ditch, he left us never a penny, and his trousers wouldn't fit any of us, so we went on east by the river. We slept that night in a hole in a ditch, and the horse we hobbled and tethered. We slept in a ditch as beggars do, and that night a Roman robbed us!'

'Robbed you?'

'Aye, robbed us. We woke in the morning, our horse was gone, and our trousers were hung in a treetop. The thief left his runes in the bark of a tree, Aristarchos the son of Demos. Let Romans rob beggars as much as they like, but they ought to stay in their own country. We weren't going to let them do it again, so we went north in a hurry. North we went in hunger and cold, for the snow had come and the winter, till up in the mountains we came to a hall that belonged to a noble named Fenris.'

'Named Fenris?' they all bawled.

'Yes, Fenris. We told him the tale of how we'd been robbed by Romans down by the river. They'd taken our horses, our silver, our gold, they'd taken our horns and our trousers. Only our swords that we slept on at night were left to show we were noble. They'd driven us out in hunger and cold to trudge our way home through the mountains, when all that we wanted was freedom to go to the east to try Scythian women. But we'll never see Scythian women now, the Polyani have got all the traffic.

'Fenris was warm-hearted and generous, the fool, and he took us into his household. He had seven fine daughters and seven strapping sons, though these last had gone off to . . . forage.'

'To forage?'

'Yes, to forage.' They passed Tyr up another sausage, he'd finished the first one.

'Now old Fenris lived well, with Amber and bronzes, wine, furs and salt fishes, with silver and salt. He lived on the Asers, though little they knew it. He bribed men and bought men, he raided, he cheated, he swam across rivers and emptied the trap lines, and all that he got he sent down

69

to the Romans, he passed it through Otho to sell at cut prices. No, he had no morals and no sense of beauty, no rings or cartels could appeal to his soul. And so he grew wealthy on crumbs from the table of great Njord Borsson, the Lord of the Asers. Drink all to the Asers, drink to great Njord Borsson.'

Everyone drank, and then of course they went back to the counter for more beer.

'Fenris had one daughter, a lass called Hedwiga, a tall wench and strapping, with skin smooth as marble. Her hair that hung braided in two yellow pigtails hung thick long and fragrant clear down to her bottom. They swayed and they bounced as she walked in the rickyard, her hips swayed, her breasts shimmered, a sight for the starving. I knew she'd come, the way she looked at me, once alone in the barn we'd soon have got . . . friendly.'

'What, friendly?'

'Yes, friendly. Another loved Ulla, and one wanted Hermod, we'd soon have been talking if not for their father. He had eyes where we had backbones, he had ears where we have toenails, he could hear the sun arising, he could see the grass a-growing, seven daughters on the rampage he could watch and never miss one. How then do you bed a woman when her father watches daily, when her father listens nightly, when she sleeps behind the hangings, and his bed's across the doorway?

'Then Hermod had a brainwave, he always was a genius, we'd get the old man drunk and pass him where he lay. Don't ever drink with Fenris, it really isn't worth it, his legs and feet are hollow, and the beer just drains away. So even drinking three to one, he had us on the floor.

'Then Hermod had a brainwave, he always was a genius, we'd tie the old man up, and let *him* sleep upon the floor. And we said that night to Fenris, when the ale horns were half empty, "Fenris, we know you are a mighty man. You walk the forest with a giant's strength. Oak trees your fingers pluck from out the earth. The winter wind is not more powerful. Has no one ever tried to bind your arms?" "Many have tried," said Fenris, "none succeeded. Tie up my arms with any cord you like and I will break it."

'So we tied him up first with a short length of fish line, thin light and strong – he broke it at once. Then we took twine that we use for the corn sheaves, doubled, re-doubled, an eightfold cord. He strained for a moment, then jerked, and behold it, the eightfold cord was snapped clean away.

'Now Fenris was fuddled and hazy with drinking, so we took some boat line as thick as my thumb. We tied him and wrapped him to look like a parcel, and all was set fair to get into bed. Then Hermod had a brainwave, he always was a genius, said, "Let's put him out, let him sit in the cold for the wolves to eat him," and when he said wolves, old Fenris went mad. He stretched and he strained, he wrenched and he wriggled, his face it went red and his wrists they went white. We three men stopped laughing, the girls they stopped giggling, and then in the silence we heard the knots burst!'

'The knots burst?'

'The knots burst, the rope burst, the hemp strands went flying, the benches went flying, and Fenris went mad. With an axe from the wall he chased us and flailed us, he splintered the tables and split all the stools. He shivered the pillars, he broke up the braziers, he cut up six rats and bisected a dog. The tables were scattered, the floor straw was scattered, and we all were scattered before that big axe. He chopped first at Ulla, overbalanced and missed him, he cut hard at Hermod and cut off – some hair. Then he went after me, all round the tables, and he hacked and he slashed and he *cut off my hand*!'

There was a moment of hush so that you could hear the rats in the roof. In German eyes, Fenris had done something unmentionable in striking a guest. It was Tyr who had behaved honourably in running away, resisting any temptation to strike back or defend himself, the very embodiment of virtuous self-control – or so we were supposed to think.

'Then in the morning we'd all got sober; they cleaned the wound and they sewed up the stump. Poor old Fenris, he *was* broken hearted, and we had to tell him what we'd been

71

about. That started him laughing, he near burst his gut. "What, sleep with my daughters, is that all you wanted? Why didn't you ask me? I'll fix it tonight."

We did it in style with the horse and the cockerel, with priest and with fire, corn mother and knife. Fenris no more raids the lands of the Asers, we pay him a pension, he stays at home. But I have a wife now, down there with the Quadi, and four healthy sons, one each time I go home.'

In the pandemonium that followed, Tyr came and sat down beside me.

'I always do this some time on the trip,' he told me in a confidential way, while a Vandal came round and poured beer for the pair of us. 'No, no, *you* don't pay here. I take half the profit on the beer sales, and a show like this always improves the trade.'

There were crowds of men around the beer counter, where the Vandals had effectively put up the price by simply not filling the horns so full.

Tyr went on:

'If things are flat tomorrow night, I'll do "How the Ash became the World Tree", profitable that one, I can manage five toasts in it. The night after, I've got something I've been working on for some time, about Loki and a horse, rather indecent, but quite funny. The next night, Asgard.'

Tyr never asked me anything, who I was or where I came from, he just accepted me as someone who had a right to be there.

The night before the packtrain reached Asgard, I said good-bye to the Saxons. They all urged me to come out to the west and visit them in their islands and marshes.

'You shall have the best seat in the hall, and the saltiest of the salt fish to make you want to drink more of our beer, the finest beer in all Germany,' said Cutha, 'and if I am not on the roads, as well I may be, mention my name to the King, or better, to the Queen.'

'Aye, better to the Queen,' they all said, and laughed; 'better to the Queen.'

11

The next day, as we rode through the pinewoods, I kept changing my place in the packtrain, and cutting across corners, both ways, through the trees, so that no one could say, 'I was the last to see him, and it was there.'

Late in the afternoon I slipped into the wood, and they did not see me go. I found a little hollow where I might sleep, fasting for I came to the judgment time of my life. But the white mare, that Loki gave me, I hobbled and turned out to graze, for she had taken no vow.

But how, unless Apollo watched and counted the days, did I choose, for that Night-Before-Asgard, the night of the Summer Solstice? All across the fields beyond the forest the fires burned, and men and girls leaped the flames till dawn.

An hour after dawn, when I knew the Saxons would be well out on the road again, I rode out of the forest. First I came to the Palisade by the trail, empty now in the morning, except for the Vandals lounging by the gate. And I knew that was not Asgard. And I turned north, at a fork, and in a hundred paces I came out of the scrub to a cluster of houses on the forward face of a ridge. But I knew this was not Asgard.

The path led through the village, past the dirty houses, to the crest of the ridge. Where the path went over the ridge, there was an ash tree on one side, and on the other a Standing Stone, raised by the Men of Old.

I smelt the sea, and that I could see a half mile from the crest. Between the ridge and the sea was a salt marsh. Down from the Standing Stone and across the marsh went a causeway of logs.

In the marsh stood Asgard. The great halls stood above the marsh, on a decking of wood, old and dry, but covered with clay that it might not burn. And this decking was carried on piles that lifted it twice the height of a man above the reeds and the brackish water. No man could come at Asgard, except along the causeway from the land, or along the jetties from the sea. Around the decking went a palisade of tarred wood. The marsh was too deep for a man to wade, and too shallow and full of reeds for a boat. No man came into Asgard unless he were asked.

Asgard

1

I laid my spear against the ash, and tied the mare to the branches. I went to a house where there was a pile of firewood already stacked, and I took it and piled it on the crest of the ridge. I led forward the mare, and I cut her throat with the edge of my spear. Her blood poured out on the ground and her breath mingled with the wind.

I struck fire from the Standing Stone with the blade of the spear, and I kindled the brushwood and the pine billets. And when the smoke of the sacrifice rose to send the mare to draw the everlasting chariot around the earth, I leant on my spear and looked at Asgard.

As I stood with the south-east sun hot on my back and the first dryness in my mouth, I saw a man come out of the gate of Asgard and walk slowly and steadily toward me. He was of middle height and thick built. He wore a mail shirt, and trousers of leather. His helm shone with bronze, and his sword hilt glittered with gold and rings. His shield was painted with an eagle, and his green cloak was worked in gold and silver thread. In his hands he carried a broken crock with a little water, and a crust of rye bread. He came to me and shouted:

'I am Heimdall that keeps the gate of Asgard. I know you, Votan Whitehair. If you come into Asgard my master Njord Borsson may let you eat the crumbs at the bottom of his table.'

But I said, 'I am Votan, the old, the young, the first, the last. Myself a sacrifice to myself, myself dedicated to myself, nine days I hung in the tree. And I tell you, I will not come into Asgard till Njord Borsson himself come out with barley bread and bitter beer to bring me in.'

And he poured out the water on the ground and threw the bread to the dogs, and he went back.

When the sun stood west of south above my head, and my throat was dry in the heat, I saw a man come out of the gate of Asgard and walk slowly and steadily toward me. He was young and golden-haired. His trousers were of blue linen and his shirt of purple silk, and his cloak of fine white wool. There were gold chains about his neck, and gold rings on his fingers. His belt was a chain of Amber links, and the handle of his knife was Amber, and the sheath was carved from one piece of Amber. In one hand he carried a glass of wine and in the other he carried a loaf of white wheaten bread. And he said:

'Votan, Spearbearer, Spearbringer, I am Frederik Njordson, and my father Njord Borsson bids you come into Asgard to dine with him.'

But I replied, 'I am Votan, born and not born, from the south and not from the south. Wounded with my own spear, nine days I hung in the tree. And I tell you, I will not come into Asgard till Njord Borsson come out himself with bitter beer and barley bread to bring me in.'

And he broke the glass of wine on the Standing Stone, and he threw the bread to the sea-gulls, and he went back.

When the level west sun shone in my eyes, and my tongue was a stick in my mouth, I saw a man come out of Asgard and walk slowly and steadily toward me. He was old and frail, a great age, fifty or more, and his hair was white as mine. His trousers were of fine wool, and black, and his tunic of fine linen and black, and his cloak of heavy wool, and black. One gold chain was about his neck, and one gold ring upon his thumb, and a gold circlet in his hair. In his hands was a silver tray, and on the tray was bitter beer in a silver cup, and barley bread on a silver plate. And he said:

'Votan, I am Njord Borsson. Lay your spear on your

76

shoulder, and bear it into Asgard and take your place among the Asers.'

I sprinkled salt upon the bread and I ate, and I drank the beer. I took Njord's right arm, and walked with him across the causeway into Asgard. To one side there were halls, and to the other side there were halls, and in front of us was the great hall of Njord, Valhall.

At the door of Valhall I bowed to Njord and I placed my spear in his hands.

'Well do we know this spear,' he said. 'It is called Gungnir. It was once a sword, a sword of heroes. Many the shields it spoiled in battle, many the heads that rolled before it. Then it grew thin and weak with much honing. Here it was beaten into a spear head, beaten by smiths of immortal cunning.' And he gave me back my spear. And I went into the hall that stood on the right of the door of Valhall, and the Vandals brought me water and lye, and they brought me clothes both grey and gay, and I washed myself and combed out my long white hair, and I dressed in grey.

I walked alone into Valhall, and the sidetables were full of men in rich clothes. Behind the top table sat Njord in a great high-backed chair, and on his left were two chairs, and on his right were two chairs.

Frederik spoke into my ear:

'Go on, Votan; take your rightful place among the Asers.'

Which was my rightful place? Not so difficult. Njord's son must sit at his right hand, so I went to the far left seat, and modestly waited to be moved higher, next to Njord. On my left hand, at right angles to me at the head of the side-table, was One-handed Tyr, and opposite him at the other sidetable was a handsome man in green called, I found, Baldur. We looked down the hall, and Heimdall with a flourish pulled back a curtain, and Freda entered.

Was there ever anyone like Freda? Well, frankly . . . no. There may have been others like Edith, and even others like Bithig, difficult though that may be to imagine. And there are ten thousand like Ursa or Gerda in every nation in Germany. But never anyone like Freda.

Freda came up the hall. She was white-clad and gleaming, golden-haired and willowy, shining and splendid in the red and yellow torchlight. Gold rings were on her fingers, gold bracelets on her arms, a great gold brooch was at her shoulder. Behind her were her maidens in yellow or green or crimson. She sat at my right hand between me and Njord.

On the table in front of Njord, Heimdall set a whetstone. A strip of stone a foot long, square, it bellied in the middle to two inches thick, narrowed to the ends. At each end it was carved with four faces under one crown, red painted, gilded. It had never sharpened sword or knife. When the whetstone was on the table, the meal began.

All in the hall ate off silver, but Njord and his children and I ate off gold. All drank from horns, gold-lipped, gold-mounted, but we drank from glass. What we ate or drank that night I cannot remember, but it was probably no different from any barbarian feast that I attended anywhere else.

For that night already I knew I must have Freda. That night she scarcely spoke, and I was drawn only by her beauty, her fragrance, her keen look, her clear grace. Later I found there was a clear mind too behind those great blue eyes, and a complex way of thought you could never guess from a few conventional phrases like, 'Have another boar's head,' or 'Please pass the chickens.' Clear, complex, but, I must admit, limited.

2

Next morning I woke in my new house, and a Vandal brought me bread and beef and beer. I went to Njord and said:

'I am, then, Votan Aser. You, great Njord, have said so. What am I to do in Asgard?'

'Come with me,' he said, 'and see what the Asers do. Whatever we do not do, that do you.'

So all day I watched what the Asers did. All day Njord sat at the gate like Loki, and as the merchants rode in and out, he spoke with them and drank with them.

Baldur rode out. In the village at the top of the ridge, and in a hundred villages, the peasants grew corn and meat for Asgard. Baldur ruled them, and they planted what he told them to plant, and they gathered it when he told them to gather it, and all went well. While the young and handsome Baldur planned, all prospered, and the peasants were well paid in silver and salt for corn and meat; for raw wool came furs and fish, and for raw hides, dyed cloth and made shoes.

One-handed Tyr rode out with a dozen Vandals. These men were themselves Captains of Vandal escorts, horsebreakers and horse-traders, and packtrain masters. Tyr ruled them, kept the palisades in order, said who should travel and who should not, and where and when.

Frederik took a gang of men down to the jetty. Some worked repairing the planking, others unloaded a ship full of salt fish. This was about Frederik's limit. Any brain in that generation had gone to Freda.

Where was Freda? She was working harder than anyone. There were always a hundred mouths in Asgard to feed, and in all the palisades. There was grain to be ground, bread to be baked, beer to be brewed, and all was done under her hands, there was nobody in the kitchens to be trusted.

Trusted? I looked at how things went in the warehouses. Njord sat at the gate, but the trading was done by a crowd of men under Skirmir. I never liked the man. I watched the way it was done, straight barter of furs against glass, Amber against silver, salt from the Saxon saltpans against wine, salted fish against pots. It was no wonder Skirmir looked so fat and dressed so well. I saw what the Asers did not, what I could do.

I talked to the three I could trust, Tyr and Freda and Njord. I asked Njord if he had bought anything himself lately, or been into the storehouses.

'No, I leave it all to Skirmir. Are you trying to say the Asers are being cheated?'

'Well, not cheating exactly. Let's call it friction. But if you look in the warehouses you see the result. Furs bought by the bale uninspected, common furs at the same price as ermine. Old-fashioned bronze winestrainers nobody will buy from us, black cloth when nobody wears black but you. And grey and dark blue, too. Whoever heard of a German wearing those colours from choice? As long as you go about things this way, by barter, there's always going to be a way for salesmen to bribe our buyers.'

'How do we stop it?' they all asked.

'There are two essential tools of business. One is writing, and the other, we'll begin with that, is . . .' I looked at them. 'Have you ever heard of money?'

And of course, they hadn't. Everything went by barter. I couldn't talk about coin, there, of course, but I could talk about weight of silver. It took me the best part of the summer to work out just what we had in the storehouses and calculate prices for everything depending on how big our stocks were. I drew everything out on the sand of the beach.

Soon the merchants began to get used to doing everything in terms of pounds weight of silver. They got used, too, to the idea that ermine was a more profitable proposition than bear, and to the fact that old-fashioned bronze buckets brought only scrap prices, and that thin wine was paid for as vinegar. And at the end of every day, each of our own dealers had to give some explanation of what he had sold, and show us what he had bought. Skirmir began to look less prosperous.

After dinner, each evening, I walked with Freda on the jetty. It is not a thing I would recommend to try in any German village. But there, Asgard was not a real German village, Freda's appearance in hall showed that. And I was Votan Aser, Old Man, Young Man, no one knew what, but very definitely a Holy Man and Freda, well, she was Freda, Njord's Daughter, and a law to herself.

We walked and talked on the jetty.

'Why do you do all this, Votan?' she asked. 'What do you want from Asgard?'

'Why, what does anyone else want from Asgard?'

'Anyone else?' she was contemptuous. 'Who else in Asgard would want what you want? Tyr or Baldur, who can think of nothing but corn and horses? Frederik, that blockhead who can't tell copper and glass from gold and diamonds?'

'There are other prizes besides gold and silver, and other Asers besides those.'

'And who has been telling you about them — Tyr?'

'I hear things from Cutha Cuthson.'

'Not much passes Cutha. Votan, Votan, why were you so long in coming?'

3

You cannot ask for a woman's hand when your own is empty. I preached constantly to the Asers the great truth that bullion is the only wealth, that gold and silver are the true aim of all trade. How then could I ask for Freda and not bring gold and silver to Asgard?

I listened to the tales the merchants told, and the songs they sang, especially the men from near the Rhine. I heard again and again the songs of the great battle in the wood, when the three legions went down. What these men told me was one thing. The things they thought I knew were quite another.

I went to Njord.

'Give me a horse,' I said. 'The God has come upon me,' and I knew that he could not deny me. The Aser horse stables were beyond the ridge, in the village. I went there with Freda and Tyr. Njord, once I had come to Asgard, never passed the Standing Stone again but once. At the stable door, with the long line of stalls in front of me, on both sides, I asked Freda to bind my eyes.

I knew I was expected to choose a white mare; this was the usual mount of a Holy Man. The mare under the Tree of the Spear had been white, and it was a white mare Loki had given me. But instead, blindfold, I walked down the aisle between the stalls, and stopped at random. Then I spun on my heel several times, and stretched out both my hands in front of me till I felt a flank. I took off the bandage myself.

81

It was a stallion, and a black, the biggest horse I ever rode on. He was fast too, some people used to say he must have eight legs he went so fast.

I put a bridle on him, and a saddle, and led him over the causeway into the gate of Asgard. Njord looked at him.

'When the spear was made,' he said, 'a mare was brought. When the mare was taken, a colt was left. This is the colt. It is Sleipnir.'

4

I rode west from Asgard. I spent a night at Orm's place, one of our palisades. There I talked with a party of Batavians. They said the same thing as all the other Germans. South and west of Orm's place was the Heath, and across the Heath no packtrain would go.

'Why not?' I asked this party, just looking for confirmation. They all answered, everybody trying to get his own little phrase into the conversation.

'It's haunted.'

'The whole place is a sacrifice.'

'Ghosts walk there.'

'Long, long ago, there was a great King, a great King, greater than all Kings. Out there on the Heath there is a tree. There he sacrificed an army.'

'Aye, with his own hand he devoted them all to the Gods. The men he killed, the horses he killed, all their weapons he broke, and their treasure he scattered before the Gods. And no living men go there.'

'How long ago?' I asked, as I so often asked, but no German has any sense of time.

'Oh, long ago, long, long ago,' they said, as usual.

'Who was the King? What was his name?' and they all went on,

'A great King.'

'Long, long ago.'

'Tall as the sky.'

'Long, long ago.'

'Tall as the sky.'

'Long, long ago.'

'His arm was strong as the sea.'

'At the beginning when the earth was formed.'

'With his own arm he sacrificed them all, thousands on thousands.'

'Long ago.'

'A great King.'

'Long, long ago.'

Once I had thought it all tales. But there were so many who told the same tales, and from so many different places. Next morning, at sunrise, in sight of them all I cast my spear into the face of the sun, into the eye of the day, and I vowed to ride to the centre of the Heath. And they all said,

'It's all right for you, look who you are. But no mortal man has ever been there since.'

I asked Orm:

'What *is* at the centre of the Heath?'

'How should I know better than you? Some say there's a tree there, and some say there's a serpent. Some say there's a dragon guarding treasure, and some say there's a hole to the centre of the world. I think there's nothing; no, not just empty land, just nothing, no sky, no land, just nothing.'

It was a bad day to start across the Heath. When I cast my spear into the eye of the sun, I had to guess where the sun might be, for the mist covered everything. You couldn't see far, and you couldn't make much speed. I wrapped my cloak around me and I made south-west as far as I could guess. About noon the sun began to break through, and I could see the kind of place I was in.

It was sandy, gravelly country. The lower places were boggy. The higher ground had some fir trees, but mostly it was heather and coarse grass. There were snakes, too; it was adder country if ever I saw it. They were out sunning themselves on the stones, everywhere. Later, there weren't any trees. There were no people, no birds or big animals. Only snakes. It was dead quiet on the empty heath. There was only Sleipnir to make a sound. Yet I heard things as I heard them on the tree. I didn't see anything, only heard them, the sound of a beaten army, men groaning and shouting, wagons creaking as they turned and twisted along roads not yet built. Pressed from all sides, they sought room and space not to fight, not even to die, but only to surrender and have rest.

When the sun was north of west and below my shoulder, I came to a boggy pool. Beyond was a plain, and in the centre of the plain, a mile in front of me, at the very centre of the Heath, was a tree. Here the silence was more silent. The beaten army had at last found its rest. The water, yellow in the evening light, looked evil, treacherous, but Sleipnir bent his head and drank. I drank too, and I filled my old water bottle. I ate some of the bread and sausage I had brought, and I wrapped myself in my grey cloak. I turned Sleipnir loose. I did not light a fire, nor in the barren place did I expect wolves or bears. I slept. In that place Apollo sent no dreams.

But in the hour before dawn, the God himself stood before me, in scarlet cloak, and breech clout, in long hair and uncut beard, as he stands in the Sanctuary in the Old City.

'Father Paeon,' I asked him, 'do I do thy will?'

He answered:

'Here in my secret place you seek me out. Take what you will to do what I will. What you will take, you will return tenfold when all I will is done.'

He went in the mists of the dawn, the dawn I could not see for mist.

After dawn I drank and ate. Sleipnir came where I knelt at the pool and nuzzled my neck. I mounted and rode toward the tree.

5

A furlong from the tree, Sleipnir stopped dead, and I could not get him to go farther. In such a case you can't make the horse go any farther, even if you get down and pull, so I dismounted and walked forward.

I walked on the things that Sleipnir would not step over. In the long grass things unseen shifted and cracked under my feet. They had been there a long time. The bones were mouldered and etched into the sour soil. The iron helmets rusted into the skulls. Here and there the bronze of armour or cloak fastenings remained, green and greasy, the leather and the cloth long rotted away.

Those bronze strips came from shield rims, oblong convex shields. These had been horses, long rows of them, little but the teeth remaining.

They all lay, men and horses, where they had fallen. Some had gone down quietly, others had writhed or struggled. But the bones were not disarranged, no wolf or bear had feasted, nor vulture nor crow. Only the adders slithered among the bones or sunned themselves on the skulls.

How had they died? No bone was smashed, no skull split, no neck severed. They had died as the white mare died at the gate of Asgard. Each had faced the tree, and then the quick slash of the knife, the hot blood on the ground and the hot breath in the air. But then not burned, nor buried, just left. With all their arms and armour, all their clothes, their boots, even their jewels, just left.

Here a heap of rusty corruption, with fragments of bronze, enamels, jewels, that had been a bundle of swords, every blade broken. That pile of old iron – that had been a mass of spear heads, the shafts broken. This was booty, the plunder from a great battle. They had brought the prizes of war to a sacred tree, and sacrificed it to Wude, to Tiwaz, to all the gods. They killed the horses, they killed the men, they broke and blunted the weapons, they hacked the leather of the shields. Here they had been the pioneers of a legion. The axe edges were turned, the saws heated and their tempers spoilt, the faces of the hammers scored with a cold chisel. In the north they would have thrown it all into a peat bog. Here they had to let it lie on the heath.

How many? The survivors of three legions. The others

85

were up in a peat bog. There had been many nations at that victory, and the plunder was shared. There *were* others, indeed. There was an eagle missing. Two standards, the shafts broken, had been left to lean against a tree.

An army is too big to hang. Some men had been hanged, though, hanged and left to rot in the air. Their bones lay in jumbled heaps on the ground; after all the years you could still see the rope marks on the bough. Not so many years, though. I had known old men who had heard at first hand about old Claudius raving through the palace when he heard, how he cried,

'Varus, Varus, bring me back my legions.'

Well that was Varus now, by the look of the jewels. Just a shapeless pile of rubbish.

Herman was dead now, that great King, whose arm was strong as the sea, who stood tall as the sky. He was no pile of rubbish. They had burned him, and perhaps the dust of his ashes had blown over Varus's bones. Now after three or four generations no one could even remember his name. He had driven the Romans back to the Rhine, he had thrust through the Marcomen to the Danube, the nearest thing to an Emperor the Germans ever had or ever will have. But all forgotten now, dead and forgotten. You have heard those tales of the long memories of people with no writing. False, all false. Who remembers Herman but his enemies?

This was no place to stay, where no wind blew, where no bird or beast moved, only the adders. Varus had a fine gold brooch, with a cameo, the Judgment of Paris. I took that for a gift. Behind the tree in an untidy mound, under the cups and mirrors and trappings of the officer's baggage, were the regimental pay-chests. Into my saddlebags I shovelled the great piles of gold coin, as much as Sleipnir could carry, as much as I could lift. From the regimental plate I took one piece I liked, a boar, silver gilt, a foot long. I went to the standards. The shafts were broken. I couldn't take everything, the crosspieces, the chains and crowns and plaques. I unscrewed the eagles themselves, and put them in my bag. Was there anything else I wanted? I could always come back for it. Only the Holy One of Wude would touch, would receive Wude's sacrifice.

6

It was most of a day and a night again and some of the next day, to Orm's place. That evening I went into the hall and sat at the centre of the high table. I could tell by the language that the room was full of Saxons, and I looked around for a face I knew. I found it and called,

'Cutha! Cutha Cuthson! Come up higher.'

He sat at my left hand, since Orm was on my right, as was only proper, it being his house.

'Well, Allfather,' he said; I was used to being called that by men twice my age and more, it is something that happens when you go white in a night. 'It is good to see you in your proper place at last.'

'All the same, Cutha, you can do something for me, or perhaps Orm can. I want a smith, a good one, a man I can trust.'

'Want one? Buy one?'

'Buy one, hire one, steal one, I don't care. And I'll want a carpenter too.'

'What kind of smith?' asked Orm. 'Blacksmith? Sword-smith?'

'No, bronze, and gold. And the gold mostly leaf beating, weeks of beating.'

'I have a nephew,' Orm said. 'He is a maker of anything, in any substance. He would go with you. For wood, look, he made this table, all that carving on the legs. And in bronze, here, Gand . . . *Gand!!* Too much noise in this hall; Gand! pass me your horn; see? Good enough? His name is Bragi.'

'He'll do you,' said Cutha. 'I knew his mother, Saxon she was. And his father is a Vandal, Orm's brother, and what more do you want?'

The Saxon half would guarantee loyalty, the Vandal half . . . well, the Vandals are a byword throughout the north for their sensitivity, their love of beautiful things, their craftsmanship. The table and the horn mount were good enough. I saw the man, and he agreed to come with me, and he brought his apprentice, Ingelri, who wasn't so good on the wood but was a promising worker in metal.

. It took us days to get back to Asgard. We worked through the forest, marking down stands of timber for charcoal. At the last we went through the woodyards and the piles of weathering timber near Asgard.

'You'll want oak for the frames, and limewood for the back and panels,' Bragi said.

'Here, this oak looks well weathered,' I told him.

'Yes, but not that branch. It's had mistletoe growing on it. You can still see the scar. You couldn't sit on that, it wouldn't be proper.'

'Take it all the same,' I told him. We kept that branch apart, and worked it down into a spear shaft, taking care that the scar showed still. Then we sweated a spear head on to it, a good one, and Bragi made a bronze ferrule, and we gave it to Loki at the next Yule. He was very pleased with it, and called it always his Mistletoe Twig.

7

That night I went into Valhall late, when I knew that Freda was already at her place. I swaggered in and I strutted up the Hall to stand before Njord. To Freda I bowed and I said,

'I bring you a brooch, costly in craftsmanship, in gold and glass cast and carved.'

To Frederik I bowed and I said,

'I bring you a boar from the bushes, gold from the Ghost Land, fetched from the forest and chivvied across the causeway.'

There was a long silence. Then I bowed to Njord, and I began,

'To you, my Father, King of the Amber Road . . .' I paused. '. . . . Before the winter is over I will give you a house of gold, and columns that glisten.'

And as I went to sit by Freda I prayed that Bragi was as good a worker as he said; and then I cursed the way that now I could hardly speak ordinary prose, but had to keep on spouting alliterative nonsense, whatever I had to do to the sense.

I looked at Freda, and I caught her eyes. I knew that she might look with interest on any fresh face in the wilderness, that you might take her ear with strange tales or make her wriggle her toes with a kiss, but the way to get at Freda's heart was to satisfy her greed. For jewels she would do anything. That great morse she pinned over her breast. And Frederik proudly placed the golden boar on the table before him, as pleased as if he had won it himself. As Njord his whetstone, so Frederik his boar. What for Votan?

I looked at Freda, and I caught her eyes. I knew I might ask for her when I would, or even take her without asking. But before I asked I had more gifts for the Asers, and they must be ready before the Amber Fleet came in.

8

Next morning, Bragi and I went through the bronze stores, and found sheets of copper, easier to work. We had some Vandals fence off a place on the ridge, and Bragi and Ingelri began to beat out copper tubes.

I went into the village and found the potter. Just as in Vindabonum, the merchants brought up Samian pots, but this was too expensive for the peasants, and they used a local gritty ware, rather nasty. The women made it themselves, and I could never persuade any of them to use a wheel. The potter, as she called herself, was the old woman who owned the kiln, and charged others for using it, and made little pottery herself, except for her own use.

I bargained with her for space in the kiln. The first pot I turned out set her quite aback. She stared at it. Then she just squashed it with her foot. Pots, she let me know, were not like that. Pots were like this . . . and she made one. I told her no. I wanted magic pots, like this, and this. Now would she please dry them in the sun, and then fire them as usual. Just to show goodwill, I'd make a couple of pots of her shape, like this . . . and she could have them to sell, or keep if she preferred. Now for more magic pots . . . no, they wouldn't hurt the kiln, or the pots in the rest of the batch. I'd make sure of that with a spell, and I recited another twenty lines of Homer. I thought Andromache's lament for Hector most appropriate in the circumstances.

That took till nearly midday. I went into the kitchens of Asgard, and found Freda. I asked her,

'Who does your brewing?'

'I do, who else? Why?'

'I want some mash.'

'Take your pick. Here's the barley mash for the beer, but over here I've got some honey fermenting, and the cranberries are nearly ready.'

I sniffed around and I decided that the honey mash, in great bronze cauldrons, was the best choice. I had it all carried off to our little place behind the ridge, Freda complaining bitterly that she hadn't meant me to take so much.

Two days later the pots were ready, and the piping, and we had a good supply of charcoal carried in. I found a couple of boys from the village to watch the pots, and we began to make . . . well, it's a temple secret, really. The trouble I had making sure that no one person ever saw all the process! It was difficult with the honey mash, up till then I'd only seen it done with grapes, but by hard work we had three jugs filled and sealed when the Amber Fleet came in.

9

There were three Amber Fleets that year. One came from Scania, across the Eastern Sea, and was led by Siggeir, King of that land and of its people, who called themselves Goths. But some of the Goths, a few generations before, had settled on an island, named Borg, and from there had spread across into Germany, on the coasts above Outgard. They called themselves after their island, Burgundians, and their Amber Fleet came in the next day, under their chief, Sigmund Volsungson.

He called himself a king, though there was a certain reluctance in some quarters to acknowledge the title, and there was, to say the least, a coolness between Siggeir and Sigmund. The Goth King resented the independent airs of the Burgundians, and there was some trouble between the two men, over a woman of course, though I never heard the details. Volsung himself had been killed in battle against Siggeir.

But in Valhall, none bore arms, and in Asgard no men might quarrel. There was no fighting or quarrelling on the quays, either. The stockade in the village was full, but not of traders. Vandal spearmen, and Lombard warriors with great axes had been dribbling in from the forest for weeks. It need never take us more than a few days to raise a small army of these hungry men, eager to earn a few pieces of silver, or, better still, grain and salt fish and cloth to help them through the winter. But without them to keep the peace, I would not have given young Sigmund's life more than two minutes' purchase, nor that of his little nation either, if Siggeir and the Goths had ever gone at them in earnest. Still, I thought, some day it might be worth knowing that Siggeir and Sigmund might so easily be brought to fight.

From Siggeir I bought a necklace carved out of ivory, walrus ivory of course, though he swore it was elephant, images of birds all joined together with gold wire. One of Sigmund's men sold me a brooch, a strange piece, not Roman, but from farther east, beyond the Scythians or India or the Silk country. The fool thought it was Gaulish, bronze was bronze to him, he sold it by weight, and stone was stone and worthless. It had a stone, not a gem, but hard stone like marble, all carved into a bird and a flower, as plain as if it were written with a pen on that stone the size of my thumbnail. Hard stone, ten years of a man's life went into carving that, and a drunken Burgundian sold it for two denarii and a horn of strong ale.

There were a few days of frantic trading, carrying up Amber and ivory from the ships, and valuing it in silver. Then we sold them what they wanted, bronze and iron, cloth and pottery, jars of wine and casks of dried fruit. Most precious of all was glass, more precious even than silver plate embossed with Gods and cupids.

On the last night, our own Gods and cupids, our gold and silver plate came out for a last feast. We pushed in more chairs at the top table to seat the Kings on either side of Njord.

Then when the whetstone lay in front of Njord, and the gold boar stood in front of Frederik, but before ale had been poured, I rose and banged my fist on the table. Then Bragi walked up the hall, carrying a tray of small silver cups that we had found at the back of the silver store; they had not sold because the Germans had nothing strong enough to be worth drinking out of them. These cups he set before the Kings and before the Asers, before Baldur and One-handed Tyr as well. Then Ingelri gave Bragi a jug, and he filled the cups.

We all eight drank. And seven of us had never drunk anything like it before, and seven of us didn't believe it. And you, of course, will never have drunk anything like it, unless you have been initiated to one of the secret Gods. It gives a glow inside, rather like drinking a charcoal brazier. You don't get it like that with wine, or from draughts of black bitter beer, even if you make the beer hot in a cauldron as the Germans like doing. When the coughing was over, I told Bragi to set them up again. We soon had two cheerful Kings and five very happy Asers.

Then Njord, who was after all not a King, though he was richer than ten Kings together, felt that with two Kings at his table he must make some kingly gesture. He flung wide his arms – well, the liquor was more than he had bargained for, and we set him on his legs again – and he made a more restrained gesture and began to speak.

'Votan Whitehair, Votan Aser, for this gift of yours, this – what d'ye call it? Honeydew? – Votan, for this Honeydew ask of the Asers any gift you like.'

This was the time to strike, and to strike with finesse, with ceremony, straight to the heart.

'Njord, great Lord of the Asers, Father of all who guard the Amber Road, as an Aser I ask of the Asers the gift of an Aser. I ask for Freda.'

Njord looked a bit taken aback. I motioned to Bragi to fill up the cups again, and to Ingelri to get another jug ready.

'This is a great thing you ask,' faltered Njord. 'To marry Freda . . . and there is Loki . . . I thought . . .'

Rather than have him stumble on till he sobered, I pushed in,

'Loki is married to Outgard, he would only take her from you. Do I not dwell here in Asgard, to see that you are not cheated? When did Loki bring you silver to double your last year's takings? Do I not heal the strains of your joints and sing you songs without number? Have I not promised a Golden House, and will I not teach you writing? The Honeydew I have poured out here, to loosen your tongues, to grant visions. Freda I ask for my bride, for my own, and in earnest I give her presents.'

And I put the ivory chain around her neck, and I fastened the bronze and stone brooch into her dress, and on her finger I put her ring, that I won from a Friesian at dice, in Orm's place, pale Irish gold with a cameo, Leda and the Swan carved on a sardonyx.

And then I might not have done it. Frederik and Sigmund sat together looking puzzled, fuddled rather, and a fine handsome pair of blockheads they were. But Tyr stood up and flung his one arm around my shoulder, and Baldur called out in that high-pitched voice of his which always irritated me,

'Oh, bother Loki, he's got so tiresome lately.'

Then Siggeir spoke, the great heavy Goth King, blue scars on his arms and face, and the authority of twenty ancestors behind him.

'You offered, Njord, you offered, you must keep your word. If the girl is willing she must go. And he shall stay here in Valhall for ever, and be an Aser till the end of time, to keep your goods and count your silver heaps.'

And Sigmund, of course, he couldn't be outdone by Siggeir, and he was too stupid to think, even, of any bargaining, but only thought he ought to say something like a King, he got up and said:

'You have spoken, great Njord, before two Kings you have promised, and your daughter, the Lady of Valhall, you must give Votan.'

Unfortunately, having both overeaten and mixed the Honeydew with great horns of beer, he chose that moment to be sick, all over Frederik. Frederik had made an especial effort to be elegant that night, and had let us know it; he was never so friendly to Sigmund after.

Siggeir ignored this interruption, for he was a King, a real one.

'Now Lady Freda, turn and face this man. Will you take him till the end of time, to be your husband? And if you will, then tell us all the day.'

Freda didn't give a clear answer. She just stood and said,

'I must have time to weave my bridal sheets, and make a bed, and heap it high with furs. There's beer to brew, and sausage, pies and ham . . . how is it there is never enough ham . . . I cannot do it under twenty days.'

There was a huge roar throughout the hall at this reluctant bride, and with a final effort at solemnity Siggeir stood again and said,

'Bridal gifts will I bring to you, gold and Amber and ivory, walrus tusks and sealskin cloaks and knives with handles of horn. But you, Votan, you have no shield. I have a shield, of limewood and leather, bossed and bound with bronze, painted and gay with colours and marked with a raven, a bird of bronze and enamel to shine in battle. A shield to protect your bride, to ward off the weather, made by a master, a shield fit for heroes, a shield fit for Votan.'

They were still trying to revive Sigmund, so Agnar Volsungson stood up. Twice the man his brother was, I was quite sorry the following year when Lyngi Siggeirson and a party of Goths and Black Danes caught him on the Amber

Shores, somewhere beyond Outgard, and killed him under an ash tree. And there lie his bones to this day, and the adders crawl through his skull, for they neither stripped him nor burnt him, but left the body, mail shirt and helmet and sword and buckler, as an offering . . . well, to me I suppose. And that very night in Valhall I saw Lyngi look at him, and mark him down for death, even while Agnar said,

'We will bring gold and bronze work, that the men of old made and buried on Bornholm. We the Volsungas of all the Burgundians are bold to burrow for bronzes.'

What he meant was that the Royal House were allowed to rob graves in Bornholm.

Then Njord, obviously feeling that he had been thoroughly compromised, called for a toast to the happy pair. Seggeir, sweating from the strains of speechmaking, relaxed from a King into a slightly drunken middle-aged gentleman, and turning to Freda began,

'Now I remember, long ago, I was young then, going hunting with your grandfather Bor Burisson, and we raised this boar . . .'

On my other side, Tyr and Lyngi were having a technical discussion as to whether a mail shirt was worth wearing for the protection it gave, being so heavy, or whether it were not better to follow the Gaulish custom and go into battle stark naked and helmless, trusting to speed and skill with sword and shield to keep your skin. The following year, of course, it was naked that Lyngi went in against Agnar, and gutted him, much, the Danes told me, to Agnar's surprise.

As a result, relieved of any necessity for conversation, I was able to look at my reflection in my beer, and say to myself,

'Well, Photinus, what have you done now? You must be mad!'

And to tell you the truth, I was mad the whole time I was beyond the frontier, and I knew it, and I knew that every single thing I did and said would have been unthinkable to any sane man.

This would have been unthinkable to ask for Freda in marriage, to marry a savage. Why did I do it? Well, to start with, Freda was really the first clean woman I had seen since Julia, and certainly the only clean woman in Asgard, the only young woman in Asgard. Then I was stealing a march on Loki, and that put me in everybody's good books, Asers, traders, even some of his own Vandals. Most of all, I had to live, and out there on the edge of the world, there were only two ways for a stranger to live, as a noble, or as a beggar. Marrying Freda, marrying an Aser, made a noble, an Aser, of me for certain.

But why should Freda have married me? She had leapt over the fire on Midsummer Eve, and asked the Gods to send her a man. The obvious man was Loki, but was Loki more than half a man? Ask Baldur.

Then I was a novelty. I was clean, to start with, I wore my pig fat with an air. I was a stranger, mysterious in many ways, with tales of far countries. And in those days, I didn't look too bad, in spite of my white hair. My face had filled out after the time on the tree, and I combed my beard. And though I walked like a young man, I had an old man's head. I had read everything any Greek had written, I knew all that any Greek ever knew, and that made me, in the eyes of the north, a man of great and unfathomable wisdom, a man of experience that no man could collect in one mortal life.

As I thought that in taking Freda, I was taking power in the north, so Freda thought that she was taking power in me, power of a kind that was never seen in Asgard. But I wasn't powerful. I was mad! Mad! And I knew it.

Ten days later, the third Amber Fleet came in, the Black Danes' fleet from the islands up in the shallow sea. King Sweyn Halffoot came himself. They had called him Sweyn Olafson till a Saxon cut off a slice of his left foot with an axe in a sea fight. Since then he had limped, but that made his hand no less heavy, and his temper was uncertain. It was as well not to mention Cutha Cuthson to him, since the Danes were pushing now toward the Saxon shores, and thought it uncivil of the Saxons to object. There was no Saxon Fleet; the Saxons, on the whole, are incompetent sailors.

Sweyn decided to stay for the wedding, after he had sent

the fleet home, and he produced a gift for Freda, a necklace of pearls; not the fresh water mussel pearls, but real oyster pearls from Britain.

Now we had a dozen boys watching the honeydew pots as they bubbled. Ingelri and a dozen of *his* apprentices beat, beat, beat all day at the gold, beating the Roman coins into great sheets, thin as silk.

Bragi was making two great chairs, thrones, one for me and one for Freda. The frames were of oak, and the panels were of limewood, the back panels and the side panels beneath the arms, carved on either side. I had Leda and the Swan on the back panel, carved from Freda's ring, and on the other side of that panel, against my back, Danae and the shower of gold, which symbolised what I was doing for Asgard. On each side piece he carved the tree, leaves and branches and acorns, and the bees and the bear and the snake in it. The end of each arm he carved into a wolf's head, snarling, life size.

On the back panel of Freda's chair, he carved Myself in the Tree, with the wolves dancing around me, and it was much admired and craftsmen came from far away to see it and copy it. The other side of that panel he worked with an Amber ship, and a distaff and a spinning wheel on the arm panels. Above each of Freda's shoulders rose the pillars of the chair, and each of the pillars ended, like the arms, in the life size head of a maiden with streaming hair. The pillars of my chair were bare.

10

How many kings will come to your wedding? Listen, how many kings came to mine.

No Vandal king came. The Vandals were poor, a few thousand starving families, too poor to afford a king. But the whole horde of Vandals came, hoping for a free meal, and we fed them all on the shore, men and women and all the children.

97

Two Lombard kings came. They themselves were very poor. One owned a sword, and looked down his nose at the other who carried only his big axe. The latter spent his time talking to any other king who would listen about the importance of keeping up the old traditions like this of having one trouser knee always patched in an odd colour. But I noticed when Baldur gave him a new pair, he wore them, without a patch. Both tried to persuade the wealthier kings to buy mercenaries from them.

A king of the Cherusci came, from beyond the Lombards. He took great pride in being sophisticated. He had once been a sergeant in an auxiliary regiment, and knew the military roads and the inns nearly as far as Milan. He spoke rather bad Latin, slowly, and he kept trying to practise it on me, which made the other kings jealous.

A king of the Friesians came. A rich king this, rich on the herring trade with Britain. He swaggered and clinked with gold chains. He threw chains around my neck and Freda's with a lordly gesture, but with one eye on the Cheruscan, who brought a hundred jars of wine. He swore it was Falernian, but it was only that filthy Gaulish stuff, not much better than ration red. Still, I don't think he knew the difference himself.

The Saxon king didn't come. He sent one of Cutha Cuthson's men with a very tactful message, saying I would understand if he did not sit at the same table as Sweyn. And since he had heard that I always wore grey, he sent me a bridal suit of dove-grey silk, and gold combs set with garnets on which he hoped that Freda would pile her hair.

Sweyn himself stayed. He rarely moved, he spent most of his life sitting on his throne or on his ship and here he always had a chair on the jetty. As a result he had grown now so fat that no horse would bear him. His main interest was in food, and he would sit all day watching the ships and chewing sausage and salt herrings to work up an appetite for supper.

Sigmund did not come. He sent another of his brothers, Gylfi; he died the next year, too, more's the pity. Sigmund, for all he was the eldest, was the runt of the litter. He asked pointedly to be excused since he was needed at home to defend Bornholm in case of an attack by Siggeir.

Siggeir came. He came with only three fast ships, having left all his other ships under Lyngi in case the Burgundians should raid Scania. He brought his Queen, Signy, and this in itself was a wonder, for the Ladies of the north seldom travel, except to their own weddings, and never by sea. But Signy said that it was unthinkable that Freda would be married with no one better than Skirmir's wife to attend her. As if Freda had not governed all the household of Asgard herself for years.

Siggeir also brought a little yellow man who was, he said, a king of the Scrawlings. This peculiar creature spoke no word of any known language, except a few conventional phrases like 'Fill 'em up' or 'Pass the herrings'. Siggeir told me that at home this man ate nothing but a kind of tame deer that gave him milk and meat and horn and leather and served him for both horse and cow. At any rate he wore clothes and shoes of deer skin, and brought us great robes and cloaks of the same material. His name sounded like Jokuhai-inen. A thin man, he ate as much as Sweyn, but it never seemed to do him any good.

Siggeir brought me the shield. A round shield, covered in leather, it had a rim of bronze worked in dragons' heads with garnet eyes. The boss was of iron, and we gilded that ourselves later, with some of the gold leaf we had over after we covered all the pillars of Valhall. Above the boss, in bronze and enamel, flew the raven Siggeir spoke of; below the boss in enamel and bronze crawled a dragon.

Loki did not come.

On the wedding day, we did everything. We leapt over the fire, and broke the jar, we killed the cock and rode the white horse, and ate bread together. We stood under the crown and we shared the cup, and followed every rite anyone present could remember. Where I should have sworn on the sword I swore on Gungnir's point, and seven kings and a queen stood witness.

When all was over we went into the hall. For the first time the kings saw the thrones. For Freda and I sat at the centre of the top table, with Tyr at my side and Signy to support the bride. But now on each pillar of my chair, one above each shoulder, were the eagles I had fetched from the Heath. All looked at them, and the Cheruscan king, who knew well enough, said in his barrack-room grunt:

'What d'ye call those? Tom tits? or black-cocks?'

And it was on the tip of my tongue to say 'carrion crows', but then I remembered the great Goth shield that hung on the wall behind me, and I said,

'No, ravens.'

So ravens they were called ever after, and they might well have been just that, for they were tarnished and black with age, and the filth of a century propped beneath a tree. King Jokuhai-inen got very excited, and babbled away in his peculiar language, and though none of us could understand a word we realised at last that he had names for the birds. The best we could make of what he said was Hoogin and Moonin, and under these gibberish titles the birds were known ever after. And all the better in that they had no meaning or history except in the mind of a Wizard King who could raise the wind when he wished; he showed us, later.

We all sat down together to the wedding feast. No expense had been spared. We had even hired a minstrel so that Blind Hod, who usually sang at our feasts, could join in the banquet without worrying about the effect of beer on his voice. We drank Honeydew from silver cups with gold-mounted horns of beer or wine for chasers. One Lombard king drank beer, to show how he clung to the old customs. The other drank wine to show he was modern in his ideas.

We ate as I never ate before in Germany. We had oysters from Britain, that came up through Friesia, and Freda found a pearl in one of hers, which was thought to be a sign of luck. We had salmon from the land of Norroway, and eels preserved in a kind of jelly, and stewed seaweed, though I did not care to try this.

There was whalemeat, and that was strange because it was

more like beef than fish, but with a rank taste to it. And a strange thing, for the whale, that huge fish that a man may take for an island at sea, has no fat at all in its body. I, who have eaten the meat, tell you that for truth.

There was wheat bread and rye bread and barley bread. By special arrangement, a bowl of wheat porridge, legionary ration style, was served to the Cheruscan sergeant-king. He threw it at the Friesian king, but missed him and it splashed over Sweyn, who licked it off his sleeve and said it was very good and please was there any more?

I had brought quite a lot of food up from Gaul. The fruit went quite well, figs, and dried plums from Illyria. Nobody else liked the olives, though, and I ate them myself, the whole barrel, as the winter went on. It took me all that time, too, to teach Freda how to fry in decent oil instead of in pig fat.

The Honeydew was a great success. I had flavoured the mash with juniper berries, which improves the taste a great deal. We gave a big cup to the minstrel, who was churning out one of the traditional stories. But under the spell of the Honeydew he, being a Batavian, gave us a highly original version of how the brave Batavians won the great Battle of the Wood, while Herman and the Thuringians only came up after all was over.

Then the Cheruscan king sang us the descent of the Lord Mithras, for he had gone as far as the Dog, but only because you couldn't get promotion any other way.

Jokuhai-inen sang and danced, beating on a little drum, hung with silver bells. None of the others knew what it meant, but I had been watching what he had been refusing, and I knew that he was dancing the Death of the Bear. For his people, once in three years only do they sacrifice the bear in truth, but they may dance the sacrifice on any great occasion when they need good fortune.

Tyr gave us again the song of how he lost his hand. He had now added a great deal of personal and genealogical material on Aristarchos, some of which was to my knowledge untrue, and the rest of which may have been no more than wishful thinking.

101

Then they called for me to sing, and I think I gave them more than they expected. I sang them of how the Lord Apollo brought to men the gifts of song and music and writing, and when they were all entranced I ended,

> Now I can impart the art of writing
> Not only for Latin or Greek or Egyptian
> But for the Gods' language, your own tongue, the
>   German,
> Let each King leave a man to stay through the winter
> And learn of Votan the secret of writing
> To return in the spring and teach all the nobles
> The signs of the Gods, the Runes of Valhall.

And so they all agreed, and each of them left behind a noble, except the two Lombard kings, who stayed themselves to save themselves the cost of their keep through the winter, as well as to watch each other. One of them offered to hire out his wife to Jokuhai-inen for the wedding night, and was furious when he found the Scrawling king had already made arrangements with the other. But his rival was even more furious to find that Jokuhai-inen had sublet her to Sweyn and not only enjoyed her himself but made a profit on the transaction.

When all had agreed that a standard runic writing was desirable, and we had drunk all the Honeydew, and the minstrel had been mutton-boned, we went in procession to my house, lit by kings as torchbearers. Signy went in to deck Freda for the bridal bed, while the men made me drink a last horn of ale, and they had a final contest among themselves as to who could drain the biggest horn at one draft. It says a lot for Siggeir's naïvety that he thought he could pass me a horn half full of beer and half of Honeydew without my noticing, but I managed to exchange horns with a Lombard king, and he was so naïve he drank it, and he was fearfully ill later in the night. So in the end only six kings saw me to my bed.

But as to what happened there, you may learn across the Styx. Whatever Ursa, or Gerda, or any of the others were, remember that Freda was my wife, and my first wife. So don't expect to hear any more about that. In spite of what came after.

102

Lands Beyond Asgard

1

That first year of my marriage to Freda, the first year of my first marriage, was the best whole year of my life, complete and without flaw. Perhaps I was in the virginity of my powers. Perhaps it was the effect of that first bitter northern winter, cooped up on our pile-based deck above the frozen marsh. It was in that year that I learned how to command kings, how to send kings to their death and kingdoms to destruction. Hear then what I did.

First, in that winter I taught men to write. Asers and kings (even if only Lombard kings) and nobles and traders all sat down before me every morning through the winter, and learnt of me how to write. Of course I could not teach them how to write in Latin, for they cannot learn Latin, their tongues are too short. So I had to make an alphabet that would fit the German sounds. It was only then that I found out how many different kinds of the German language there are, and how many sounds. And, of course, I could not think of using wax tablets. I had to make letters that could be scratched on limewood panels across the grain.

Njord never learnt the trick at all. One of the Lombard kings was nearly as bad. The other learnt very quickly; his name was Hoenir. He had very little to do but work, for his wife, having tasted the sweets of wealth with Sweyn and Jokuhai-inen, had gone off with the Cheruscan king. He passed her on to other military friends, and when I saw her again a few years later, in Rome, she was mistress to a captain in the Praetorian Guard, and doing well on selling permits to beg around the Milvian bridge.

Loki came at Yule. He learnt to read in three weeks. This is their winter festival, when their custom is to burn a tree. This was difficult in Asgard, living as we did on a wooden deck above the swamp, in wooden houses, but I had Bragi make a great tray of bronze and we piled a heap of earth to put it on and we burnt the tree in that.

We gave Loki his spear, and he was very pleased. He made no comment on the thrones, or on the marriage, till midway through the Yule dinner, when he produced a complete set of silver plate, cups, dishes, wine strainers, bowls, two of everything, all Syrian by the workmanship, and not more than ten years old by the style. I often wondered where he stole it. Still, it was a magnificent gift.

When the banquet was well under way, he tried to feed Hoogin and Moonin with crumbs. Then he got maudlin over the maidens on Freda's chair, and called them his little Greek girls. And he used the Greek word too, Kyria, and then he called them Valhall Kyria, and the name stuck.

2

Among the men who had come in the ships with Sweyn was a noble named Starkadder. He stayed to learn the Runes, having nowhere else to go that winter but Sweyn's hall, and ours was as good. He was a landless man, having lost his farm at dice, as so often happens. One night, in the hall, I sang the tale of Scylla and Charybdis, translating Homer as best I could. Starkadder was most impressed by my description of an octopus, for they do not live in the seas of the north.

He went away next day, and repainted his shield, which before had had the usual simple design of an eagle or a boar or some such thing. He painted on it what he thought an octopus might be. There was a human face, and from it there came out in all directions eight human arms, and each of these arms carried a weapon, one a sword, another a hammer,

104

another an axe, and so on. The result was most distinctive, and ever after he was known as Starkadder Eightarms.

He came to me and said,

'Votan Whitehair, that came out of the forest with your spear on your shoulder and now sit in Asgard a Lord of the Amber Road, tell me how I too may win wealth.'

'First,' I told him, 'remember you are not Votan Spear-bearer.'

'True,' he answered, 'but I do not wish to be as wealthy as you.'

Therefore I told him how he might become a wealthy man, and I lent him silver, for there is little you can do without capital unless you are the manifestation of some God. What I told him, and how he did it, you shall hear, but it was about this time, in the winter, that I began to learn my power over kings and nations.

3

Donar came in March. He just walked into Valhall one evening just as we sat down to dinner. He came in through the door, and bellowed,

'I am Donar. I bring the sword I promised.'

He walked up the hall and laid the blade on the table in front of me. Then he went around to the seat on the other side of Njord, where Loki usually sat, and settled down in it comfortably. Nobody said a word against him. He never gave any explanation of why he had come.

The sword he brought was, of course, not a whole sword but only a blade, and the tang of the hilt. Donar and Bragi worked together on the hilt, carving it in beechwood to fit my hand, and balancing it to suit my grip exactly. However I would not let them make any rings or healing stones for it. I told them,

'There will be no healing of any blow that I strike with Votan's sword.'

Yet the blade never tasted blood but the one time, while I had it.

Donar also had for me my old sword, my Kopis. He was not very polite about the quality of the blade. I didn't know what to do with it, and in the end I gave it away, to Sigmund, when he came for a few days in the spring, trying to get credit in corn against the winter's Amber sales. He was very grateful, the blockhead, incredulous that I should give him my own sword, a sword of Votan's for his own.

I asked Donar how he had got it, indeed how he had got here at all.

'When you shouted,' he told me, 'I went into the woods. I heard one horse go off after a bit, and that must have been you. There was a lot of noise, and a great deal of cursing when they tried to scrape the burning wood out of the hut, and sort through it for the silver. After a bit lying watching them I found out there was someone alongside me. It was Occa. He had gone back a few hours, and met Wolf, who was coming up behind, as, apparently, had already been arranged. I knew there'd be somebody, but they didn't tell me. Wolf had a crowd of men, Vandals as well as Quadi, and his son-in-law too.'

'Who's Wolf's son-in-law?'

'Tyr, of course. Didn't you know, Fenris Wolf cut off his hand? Well, we came up in a circle and rushed them about dawn, but of course we couldn't hold the Vandals back and they killed the lot. We got the silver out and traded it through Tyr, and shipped a fair amount of Amber back to Otho.'

'Do you mean to say that Tyr knew I was coming?'

'Well, we heard some things from the Polyani. The real worry was in case you got to Outgard before Tyr, and you did, but we hear you took care of yourself.'

'And who else knows all this besides Tyr?'

'And what should Tyr know, other than that you are Votan Spearbearer Spearbringer, the marked of Joy?'

No more would he say. And as always around everything I did, everywhere I went in the north, there was the strange feeling that I was expected, that all was prepared, that I was playing a part in a piece I had not written, no, nor yet read.

Donar settled down, as I said, and not only in that seat, but in Asgard. He put up a smithy by the Honeydew sheds, where twenty men watched the pots, and he began to make swords, snake swords. Ingelri left Bragi and went to work under Donar, learning how to make the long ribbons of iron, and interlace them, beating them in the heat of the charcoal. So much charcoal did we need for this that the Lombard axes began to eat visibly into the edge of the great forest. Ingelri became a great swordsmith, and his swords became as famous as Donar's. More famous, because Ingelri, and all his clan, marked the blades with his name, while Donar never learned my Runes.

Donar's own sword was a Sax, a lovely thing. Instead of Runes, he inlaid the blade with patterns in silver and copper wire.

4

One day I went into the hall and Njord said to me,

'Learn now how hard it is to be an Aser. See here these men who come from Sweyn. They say that the Saxons are seizing their saltpans and driving them from their pastures, and Sweyn wishes me to stop trading with the Saxons. And these men come from Edwin the Saxon King, and they say that the Black Danes are seizing their saltpans and driving them from their pastures; and Edwin wishes me to stop trading with the Danes. What then shall I do?'

'Go to your kings,' I told the envoys, 'and tell them that in three weeks from today they will meet me at – are there any sacred places in Denmark?'

'Dozens,' said Hoenir the Lombard, and named one at random.

'Then in three weeks King Hoenir and I will meet King Sweyn and King Edwin there, and we will come to an agreement. And you, Hoenir, will bring fifty of your axemen, and you will stand as witness of any agreement and guard us all while we talk.'

And Njord did not object though I said all this without consulting him in the slightest. He merely said later that he was glad I was going, since he was no longer able to ride, and he did not want Asgard full of kings all through the summer.

I went with Hoenir and fifty of his Lombards, all riding horses borrowed from the Aser stables, much to the dissatisfaction of Tyr who protested that he could not see how to plan the summer's packtrains if he were fifty horses short.

These were hungry men with hungry axes, who left behind hungry wives and hungry children, and who, now the ploughing was over, rode with me to save the food at home, and live on the Asers. We went across the hungry land and we lived on the dry bread and bacon in our saddle bags, and we came to the meeting place.

It was some way from the edge of the woods. There was, of course, a sacred tree, and a little way from it there was a bog. The Lombards cut down young trees and made houses thatched with the green leaves. All the time I was there until the last night I ate no food that a Lombard had not prepared, and drank nothing but water from a spring that trickled down into the bog, and spoke to no one except in Hoenir's hearing.

Three days before the appointed time there came two parties, of Black Danes and of Saxons, and each party brought wagon loads of ready cut timber to build a hall, and the first task I had, and that a hard one, was to persuade them to put all the wood together and build one hall, and not two.

On the appointed day, all the common people went away, except two nobles, one a Black Dane and one a Saxon, who stayed to be witness, and the Lombards took their swords from them, and then spread out in a great circle around to keep the kings safe.

Midway through the morning we saw the kings coming, from opposite directions. Edwin the Saxon King came on horseback, and he was forced to ride in circles to waste time and not arrive before Sweyn, who sat in an ox cart. Edwin was an old man, as old as Njord, and frail.

108

There was a table and benches. I sat at the head, with Sweyn at my left hand and Edwin at my right. Hoenir sat at the foot, and the Danish noble between him and Edwin, and the Saxon noble opposite him. And I faced to the north-west, so that each king faced his own kingdom.

I avoided any question of priority in speech. I made them throw dice. Sweyn threw a five and a two against two threes, and launched into an oration. It was long and flowery, and he had obviously taken notice of Siggeir's style. He spoke for two hours, and at the end I said,

'Hoenir has written down in Runes what this great king has said. Let us hear it.'

Hoenir cleared his throat and read,

'King Sweyn said the salt beaches were empty when the Danes came. The pastures have paid homage to the Danes from time immemorial.'

King Edwin took the hint. He only spoke for twenty minutes. Hoenir read from his tablets,

'King Edwin said the pastures were empty when the Saxons came. The Saxons have made salt on the beaches from time immemorial.'

I began to question the Kings. How much salt came from the beaches? Whence came the wood to burn to make it? How many cattle grazed the pastures? Who sold the hides, and to whom? How many men? What service? What duty? What protection?

When Hoenir had everything written on his tablets I clapped my hands and a Lombard came with six silver cups and a jug of Honeydew. I poured a drop, a notional gesture, into each cup. We drank, after I had spilled a little on the table in the face of the sun. Then Hoenir and I went apart to another table. I took the jug.

We read the tablets. We talked in whispers. We drank. The others watched us in silence, their tongues hanging out. When I was satisfied, Hoenir wrote down my judgment, three times. Then we went back taking our two full cups. I left the jug.

'Hear my judgment,' I told them. 'Hoenir has written it

three times, once for Danes, once for Saxons, once for himself as a witness. Tonight I will read it to all your nobles at the feast.'

'No feast,' said Sweyn. 'He killed two of my brothers.'

'No feast,' said Edwin. 'He killed my only son.'

I sniffed the liquor in my cup. I breathed drink at them.

'There will be no more killing of kings' sons, or of kings' brothers, or of anyone else. Here is a treaty that will keep peace in the north for a thousand years.'

The two kings looked at the jug. They said they would accept my judgment.

'Hear this! The salt beaches belong to Edwin. Sweyn's men may make salt there. Edwin shall send a noble to watch, and one-tenth of all the salt shall be Edwin's, and he may take it, or Sweyn may redeem it for silver.

'The pastures belong to Sweyn. The Saxons shall graze them. Four years in five shall they pay tribute in hides and men to Edwin, and one year in five to Sweyn, but never shall they march to war for Dane against Saxon, or for Saxon against Black Dane.'

Because this judgment was complex and gave each king the shadow of his ancient title, though the substance was gone, they hailed it as a work of genius. We stood and collected the cups and I poured out the Honeydew, full cups this time, and we all drank to the treaty.

Then the Saxons and Danes came and passed the axe ring and brought sacrifices to seal the treaty. Silver and Amber and furs and bronze they brought, and they threw it all into the bog. They brought two men that had been shipwrecked, the Saxons had a Friesian and the Danes a Goth, and these first they hanged from the tree, and then threw still choking into the bog. And, most magnificent of all, each side brought two white mares, and the four they drove into the bog, and cut their throats as they struggled, and their blood poured out on the ground, and their breath mingled with the wind.

Then, as evening came on, tables were set up for a feast, for both sides had come prepared for a feast, however the kings had objected. I set Hoenir at the head of the high table, with the other kings seated on the sides toward their own kingdoms, and I sat opposite Hoenir, and we ate, and drank beer and Honeydew. And later I moved around among the other nobles, and I learnt many things. Sweyn wanted salt beaches so that he need no longer pay the Saxons for his salt herrings, but sell them himself to the Goths and take Edwin's trade. Edwin wanted the pastures, not for cattle, but so that Cutha Cuthson his man could raise more horses for his packtrains, and not have to buy them from the Black Danes.

When the feast had lasted a long time, an hour before dawn, I went away and passed the axe ring, and I came to the edge of the bog where no man went at night. There the Most Holy One stood before me, as He stands in the sanctuary in the Old City. His cloak was of scarlet, and His hair hung about His shoulders as did my own.

After a while I said,

'Father Paeon, do I do your will?'

He answered,

'All that I wish you to do you have done, and strife do you bring on them that are at peace. This treaty will mean war in the north for a thousand years.'

Both Saxons and Danes pressed us to come back with them. But Hoenir, much on his dignity, said,

'Two kings have the Lombard nation, and only one is at home, yet both must watch the ripening wheat or shall no harvest come.'

The greater kings loaded Hoenir with silver and Amber, and Edwin gave him a great sword, a good sword but two-edged and so quite out of fashion among the Saxons. There the people live among the islands in the marshes, and the sax with its one sharp edge and one blunt is what they need, for cutting reeds as well as for lopping heads, and for breaking lobster shells as well as for breaking bones. So Sweyn gave him a fine shield, good for land fighting but too heavy a thing to strap to your arm at sea. And every Lombard who came on a borrowed Aser horse went back leading it, and riding his own.

But I would take no fee for my judgment.

111

5

Asgard was boring in summer. Freda was pregnant. There was little to do. I took to riding off into the forest, to the villages. Sometimes I followed the packtrains, sometimes not. Wherever I went, people came to me to have their twisted bones and sprained joints put back into shape. They shared with me their food of acorn bread and salt meat. I began to learn all that went on in the north. People said later that it was my ravens that told me all I knew. It was not; it was those same people themselves, a word here, a phrase there, a change in prices, a move of a clan from one part of the forest to another.

About midsummer, or a little later, two Vandals came to me, and said that Starkadder Eightarms had what I wanted if I would come to get it, at a harbour in the Black Danes' country. So I went with them, and I found Starkadder in a rare good humour. He had done as I had told him, and now he had for me my share of the proceeds.

Starkadder had borrowed a ship from a Danish noble, one of the Amber Hunters, a man for whom he had once done a murder but who had not yet paid him. So that this man, out of fear, could not deny Starkadder the use of a ship for one voyage, without any fee. Starkadder with the silver I had lent him was able to gather a band of men, all landless men like himself, Vandals whom even the Asers would not hire, and Lombards who had quarrelled with both their kings, and Saxons and Black Danes, and Scrawlings who had come west to make their fortune, and lost their honour which was all they ever had, and men from Gaul who had come out of the Empire to save their skins, for they never had any honour. They were all men who would kill you for a penny, or sack a town for sixpence.

They took the ship and they caulked her, for she was old and leaky, and they put in some food, but not a lot for they had not much money even then, and they did not want to take anything they might have to bring back. Then they took her to sea, and they worked her north, overloaded, to the coast of the Land of Norroway.

Now whether the Land of Norroway is a part of Germany or an island no man knows, but if the shallow sea balances our central sea, as it must if there is any logic on the earth, then that great desert land, where a man may walk to Scania, must be a Northern Africa. And that is why there are elephants in the north that burrow beneath the earth to escape the cold.

They made the coast of the Land of Norroway, and they were glad to see it, and thought it more than they had hoped to do. They rowed along the coast till they came to King Vikar's hall, where it stood over a large village, on a harbour. There they beached the ship, and half of Starkadder's men came to the shore, but the rest stayed hidden under the bulwarks, and a Scrawling watchman kept everyone away.

King Vikar knew Starkadder as a hard man to have work for you, a man to send to collect your debts. Starkadder had been the King's man once, and eaten his bread, and in his band had learnt the arts of war. When the King saw it was Starkadder, he was pleased, not afraid, and bade him and his men feast in his hall. Starkadder told him that they had been on their way to raid the Scrawlings on the Amber beaches, but that they had been deceived in the mists. King Vikar thought he might have use for Starkadder, and wanted him to go north, and raid another king who had been interfering with Vikar's herring fisheries.

They sat down in the hall, Vikar's men and Starkadder's men together, one and one. Vikar's two daughters carried round the ale, Alfhilda, and Gambara that should have married Harold Edwinson. After the ale had gone round, and Vikar's men had drunk much, and Starkadder's men had drunk little, and I do not know how he managed that, Starkadder brought out four jars of Honeydew that I had given him; his hardest task on the voyage had been to stop his men from drinking it. The Honeydew they poured into the horns of King Vikar and his men.

Then they began to play the games that the Germans like to play after their dinner, and one of Starkadder's men slipped out to give the signal to the ships. It was only twilight, for it was the night before the Midsummer feast.

Starkadder said to King Vikar,

'We have a new game. We call it the game of Votan.'

'What kind of game is that?' asked King Vikar.

'First,' Starkadder told him, 'you must stand with one foot on the table and the other on a bronze bucket.'

'So I will,' said Vikar laughing. 'Bring a bucket,' for if you tell them it is a game these men will submit to any kind of indignity.

'Now you must take a live cockerel in your right hand and a horn brimful of ale in your left.'

King Vikar did so, and in the twilight the men from the ship were coming ashore into the village, with their swords drawn, and ropes coiled round their waists, and their bare axes held before them, axes with two foot blades and cherry wood handles.

'Now,' said Starkadder. 'Let your two principal chiefs make a rope of twisted juniper withies, and put it around your neck,' and this too Vikar had them do, not thinking any harm.

'Now, when I call GO! you must drink the horn of beer at one draught, not spilling a drop nor letting go the cock nor touching the withies with your neck. And I wager you a jar of Honeydew to a piece of silver that you cannot do it.'

'Done,' said Vikar, for he thought that more complex and absurd the rules, the more likely it was to be a game of skill, worthy of a king, that called for no exertion, but only for dexterity. And now the men from the ships stood all round the hall.

'Go!' said Starkadder Eightarms, and the King began to drink the beer. Then 'Pull!' said Starkadder to the two principal chiefs, and they, overbalancing with laughter, pulled, for they thought it a trick to make the King spill his beer. The King choked and let go the cock as he tried to keep his balance with his face in the horn, and his men laughed and they all watched the cock as it fluttered up to

114

the rafters. Then each of Starkadder's men took the knife with which he cut his meat, that King Vikar had laid before him, and killed his neighbour, King Vikar's man, and Starkadder took a spear from the wall, and said, 'Now I give you to Votan.' And he thrust the King through the body, and then killed the two principal men, so that their blood flowed on the ground and their breath went up into the air.

Then Starkadder and his men went through the village and every man that they found they killed, that there might not be a blood feud against them. But all the women and the boys they drove together, and they collected all the gold and silver and bronze, all the furs and amber, for Vikar was a rich King, and fit to marry his daughter to the Saxon King's son.

The next day they took King Vikar's ships, and they filled them with prisoners and booty, and they put to sea. The houses, and the corn they could not carry, they burnt. It was midsummer night, and they left only the old women and the babies to leap over the flames.

Then in a day and a night, with a good north wind so that they dared to set the sails, and women and boys in plenty to row, they came down to the harbour where I met them, and which belonged to a trader called Elesa. There they sold all the booty and the people to Elesa, and the ships too, and Starkadder took half and his men half. Starkadder never owned land, for no one would sell it him, nor would any king take his oath or hire him for more than one voyage at a time; for he had sworn an oath to King Vikar.

I went with Starkadder to see my share of the plunder, four young women, and one of them was Gambara, Vikar's daughter. I took Gambara to bed that night, but she was so much trouble and so much fuss, that I quite lost my patience with her and told her I would sell her to a brothel in Gaul. After that I went out, and it was an hour before dawn.

The God stood before me as he stands in the Temple in the Old City, in scarlet cloak and his hair about his shoulders. I asked him,

'Father Paeon, have I done what you wished?'

He answered:

'I sent you to bring destruction to the north. Now the seed is sown, and the breeze has begun to blow.'

In the end I got rid of Gambara. I did not dare take her back to Asgard. I told off a couple of Vandals to take her down as a present for Hoenir, whose wife had gone off with the Cheruscan. Now he had a sword, he was pleased enough to have a wife, and a genuine princess at that, even though her royal father ruled over a fish market, died drunk and was flung on a midden. She never showed me the least malice afterwards. Why should she? A maidenhead she was bound to lose anyway was small price to pay for a kingdom, especially since till the Vandals rolled her still bound on Hoenir's floor she thought she was bound for the brothel.

That, I said, was in the midsummer, and in the Spring she gave birth to two sons, Ibor and Agio. When they were of age, Hoenir died, and the other Lombard king came to the funeral. They killed him and his sons, and the heads they threw on the pyre. So the Lombards had two kings of the one blood, and that fresh blood, to hold against the Vandals who pressed them hard from the east. How the Vandals found a king I shall tell you later.

The other three women I took home for Freda, since I thought it wrong she should be less well served than Julia Scapella, and have only Skirmir's wife and a few village girls to do her hair. Freda was delighted, and after she had flogged each of them a few times they became quite devoted to her.

Donar, however, was for some reason most displeased at this story, and let it be widely known, so that Starkadder came no more to Asgard, but kept the seas all the summer in King Vikar's own ship, which was a good one, and in the winter he would go down into the Empire to sell his goods among the Gauls. Alfhilda, Vikar's daughter, he kept with him in his ship.

Donar spent a great deal of our silver in buying back King Vikar's people. Gambara did the same, but what she spent was mostly Lombard blood. Most of the youths and some of the women came back at the last to found a new

116

nation, though a few of the little boys had been gelded.

It was these youths and their sons who years later caught Starkadder on a lee shore on the amber beaches and killed him and all his men. Alfhilda, who had gone with him willingly on all his voyages, they threw into the ship and burnt, and her children with her, and that satisfied Gambara, who was always jealous. But Starkadder Eightarms they flung dead into the waves for the fishes to eat.

6

After the death of King Vikar, Donar had little to say to me. He seemed bored even with making swords; Ingelri was perfectly capable now of looking after their production. Donar spent a lot of time playing with Freda, and then, when the Amber Fleets came, he went away. All the kings came that year. Only Sigmund did not come, sending one of his brothers, Synfiotli. Even Edwin came, early, with shiploads of salt and salted fish. Sweyn came, wearing King Vikar's chain, for that was his price, but Donar did not know. Siggeir came, but Signy stayed at home, for she was near her time, and for once it had nothing to do with me.

Last of all, Jokuhai-inen came in his own ship. That is to say, he did not come in Siggeir's fleet, but he had hired a Goth ship, and had mixed Scrawling spearmen in among the rowers to guard his cargo of walrus ivory and sealskins. For walrus ivory we had put up the price, and it was worth his while to come himself.

He had brought a gift for Freda, a gift of a Scrawling woman. Not of his own kind, but from somewhere farther east, sallow faced and flat chested, with coarse black hair, but good sport, I tell you that, who know. But Jokuhai-inen brought one and took one, for he persuaded Donar to go back to the north in his ship with him. Donar tried to tell us all why.

'Somewhere up in that land, they say, dwells the Smith God, in a land where fire spouts from the earth and the rivers

117

run hot with steam.' That sounded reasonable enough, for there must be a burning mountain in the north to balance Etna in the logic of the world. But who would want to live in a natural hypocaust?

'So,' Donar went on, 'I will go up there and worship. Then Jokuhai-inen says he will teach me how to catch fish that swim in ice, and trap wild foxes, and milk deer. Up there the nights are half a year long. Think what feasts one can have. How much Honeydew ought I to take for a half-year's feast?'

How Jokuhai-inen told him all that I never knew, for then Donar hardly had two words of the Scrawlings' language, though when he came back he was fluent, and he had learnt it in the best place, in bed. How much sport there must be in bed when each night is half a year long!

We saw Donar go, in Jokuhai-inen's ship. The King sat at the steering oar, much to the dismay of the Goth shipmaster, who protested that Jokuhai-inen had hardly spent two hours in control, and he was sure to run her ashore or foul a jetty or ram another ship. Donar said it would be all right, for he would stand in the bow and beat out the time for the rowers with his hammer on the side of the ship. What *he* knew about it we couldn't guess. He knew only one rate of striking, and he soon had the rowers panting. We cheered and waved and they cheered and waved and the ship heavy laden wallowed out from us into the open sea. And winter came.

7

At the beginning of the winter, when the snow begins to fall, and the cattle are brought in from the forest to the byres to live, if they can, through the winter, the Barbarians keep the Feast of the Dead. This is not a feast of joy, to thank the Dead for their gift of life. It is a feast of fear, when the Dead prowl around the house, and the noise of the feast grows high to drown the noise of the dead feet outside. And games are played, as crazy as the game that killed King Vikar, so that mirth for a moment will

118

whelm the noise of the Dead, the fear of Death.

Yet all that bitter night, the doors of the hall stay open, that the Dead may come in. At the end of Valhall we placed a table, and on that table the plate was of gold and the cups of glass. There was the strongest of the beer, and the whitest of the bread, and the fattest of the meat, and the sweetest of the honey. All this was set out for the Dead to eat. King Vikar, and Grude, and the Cat king's men, and the men they threw in the bog, all dead, dead, dead, and all eating in Valhall.

Then as the minstrel was singing a cheerful doggerel, and the boys were ducking for apples, and everyone was laughing for fear that they might scream in terror, someone did scream in terror and something came into the hall out of the Night of the Dead. The noise stopped as a man's voice stops when the water goes over him. There was a long silence as it stood there, bulky and bloated and white with furs and with snow.

Then while the hall sat in silence, great Valhall sheeted with gold and hung with shields, so silent that the fire ceased to crackle and the straw to rustle, and the very rats in the roof stopped running, the being at the door raised his arm and put back his fur hood. And we should have known that no man but an Aser would have walked abroad on the Night of the Dead, and no Aser but Loki. Yet such was the shock of his entry that it was still in silence that he walked up Valhall, past the silent benches and the silent fires. And the very smell that came to us was not the smell of wet furs but the smell of death.

Four of the Great Asers sat on the top table, Njord and Frederik and Freda and I. At the sidetable nearest the High Table sat the lesser Asers. At my left hand sat One-handed Tyr, and next him Bragi, and his new wife Idun that he had only lately brought in from her village. Opposite Tyr sat Baldur, with his arm around Blind Hod, and between Frederik and Baldur was an empty chair. Not the chair that had been there when I first came to the hall, but one carved and patterned with tongs and hammers and anvils and all the instruments of a smith's art.

119

Loki then entered the hall, for the first time since Yule. In silence he walked up the hall, past the silent packmen and traders, to the silent Asers, toward the silent High Table and the empty chair. And when he was within three paces of it, when he had only to pass between the tables and take it, someone spoke: Bragi spoke:

'That is Donar's chair.'

Loki stopped, short, rigid, his body bowed a little forward, toward the chair that he had almost reached. Then he straightened up very slowly, and he turned to look at Bragi while a man might count five, slowly.

Let me tell you, that in all my years on land and sea, I have never heard language like Loki used that night. I never did find out what some of the words meant. I may have learnt some German. I certainly learnt a lot about the Asers, and I did not enjoy hearing it. He didn't take long over Bragi. I can't remember the exact words, but the gist of it was,

'And who are you to tell me where to sit, you stupid little Vandal turd? There you sit, chip-chop, chip-chop, all day, and stuff yourself all day with crusts from your betters' table. What do you think you can puff yourself up into? Whoever heard of a carpenter who behaved like a human being? And that bag from the forest with you, heather still growing between her toes, enough dirt there for an oak. Had she ever seen a plate before she came here? And now she dines off silver. There she is, cramming herself. Look at her, with her mouth full, and open too. Wind change, dear?'

Hod was unwise enough to snigger.

'And that blind beggar, harping for ha'pence on the heath he was, never a rag to his back, and even the harp he pawned for a muttonbone and stole it back again in the dark when all men are blind. And who dragged him here like a rat to gnaw at out stores?'

He spat at Baldur and missed.

'You great hermaphroditic bastard, there you sit, shame on you, cuddling him in front of everyone. Once the Spring comes, off you'll go, waggling your fat buttocks around the villages, and as long as it's young and fresh you'll take it.'

In truth, this spite was at the root of all.

'Fertility blessings, indeed, any field'll crop if you manure it. Don't like me saying that, do you? And who's going to stop me? Not that fat drunken slob at the gate, snoring like a pig, deserter from the baggage line of some second-rate legion, he couldn't guard a pot of ale.'

Yet Heimdall had come softly into the hall not five paces behind Loki, and now he stood at the door and brought his spear up ready to throw. But Njord moved his finger and the spear came down again. Loki had never noticed, he had rounded on Tyr, and here he really let himself go. He flung at Tyr a stream of precise and circumstantial accusations, a highway robbery here, a rape there, a kidnapping at this place, a merchant who was never seen again after that.

'And your hand, how do you say you lost that? Bitten off by a Wolf? Cut off for theft, more likely. Steal a bone from a dog, a crust from a child, steal anything you like, and not even because you want it, but only because it is there to steal. And as for you, you great stupid block' – this was to Frederik – 'can't count, can't read, can't think, can't fight, can't talk, what use are you to the Asers? What good are you to the world? What good are you to anybody but your father, and only good to him to remind him that once only he played a man's part.'

He spat again, on the Whetstone.

'Njord Borsson, Lord of the dust of the Amber Road! You vain old man, you sit there stroking your beard and looking fine. What do you think you are? You think that because you are the eldest of the Asers you are the greatest of the Asers, that you are the strongest of the Asers. Once indeed you were the strongest of the Asers, when you drove out Bergelmir, when you sent Mymir to drown on the winter sea. Now you are the weakest of the Asers, your strength is gone, you can turn no one out. What are you good for now but to sit at the gate and drink the liquor better men make? For ten years now you have not walked on your own feet. *She* has held you up!

'And look at her, all of you, look at her, where she sits,

loaded with rings, hung with gold chains, in linens and silks and furs. How did she get them? Don't you all know? If you want any special favours, any cheap rates, any cut prices, go to Freda, she'll fix the old man. It's no good offering just any silver or bronze or gold; but something to wear, jewels or foreign cloth . . . anything, she'll do anything. And if you had something really fine, and there wasn't anything else you really wanted, you could have Freda herself. Hands up any man, Aser or Vandal or serf, who hasn't had Freda? Any man in the Hall? Any man in all Germany? Tyr? Baldur? Heimdall? even Frederik?

'And there Votan sits by her, the fatherless man, come out of the forest from nowhere to be a professional cuckold for the sake of a free dinner every night, come down like a monkey out of the tree to sponge on old monkey Njord. And what's he do for it? He'll give you Honeydew free, and have the shirt off your back, and the skin too, while you sleep it off. He'll not kill himself, but he'll arrange your death for you, as long as he makes a penny profit. And he'll arrange a peace treaty that brings in a hundred years of war, and then he'll sell swords to both sides, and buy in the plunder, cheap. And in between – look at the randy stallion of the Shallow Sea, and watch for your wives. He wants to have as many loves as Freda, but his taste is better; *he* goes for queens. Mark him well. At the end he will bring down Asgard on your heads; but on your heads, not on his.'

And with that he turned and walked down the hall, to leave us all still and silent as if nothing had happened, as if his speech had taken no time at all. Unfortunately his dignity could not resist temptation, and he paused on the way to spit copiously, and, now having had some practice, in Skirmir's eye. That broke the tension and, the tight drumskin of the air once pierced, it was Baldur who stood up and screamed in his high voice.

'And what if Votan has slept with a thousand women? What if every one of us has slept with her? When did you ever sleep with a woman? Or with a grown man, come to that? Little boys are more your line, that can't argue, or worse, the wild beasts of the forest. Are the cattle of Outgard safe? Loki! Who fathered Sleipnir on the Mare?'

Everyone laughed. They laughed and laughed, they beat their hands on the benches, drunk or sober they shouted, they hooted, they rolled about and fell backward. In that gust of laughter, they forgave Loki his blistering scorn. Perhaps I was too sophisticated for that kind of humour, and Loki didn't find it very funny either.

He stood glaring at us all, white-cheeked. Then he did something that checked all laughter, that shook us all into a shocked and frightened silence. Loki sat at the table of the Dead. He drank the wine of the Dead, and he ate the Dead men's bread. He drank of every cup, and he ate of every dish. He poured out the beer of the Dead, and he tore the Dead men's meat with his fingers, as he ate the Meal without Salt, the Meal without Iron, the Meal of Old Time. With every bite, with every sip, he cursed us all, he cursed Asgard, silently, without a word, to death, to misery and poverty and death, death, death.

He went from the hall. Next day there were those who said that he had not come by any mortal means, that he left no footmark in the snow, coming or going. That may well have been true, in that the falling snow covered up any marks he may have made. But from that moment, when Loki went through the door, though we did not see it at once, all our luck left us, and all the threads of our destruction began to draw together.

All that Loki had done, and that was enough, was, not even to tell the truth, but only to shout aloud what each of us knew already in his heart. Who cared where Tyr had lost his hand? Better to say he lost it in a drunken brawl than under the gallows. Better to talk of faith and chastity and honour even if we know of lies and theft and adultery. Once you burrow to see the foundations, the whole wall falls on you.

8

When Donar came back in the spring, the paint was back on our faces, and the lies were true again. Again we were the great Asers, wise and good and rich, and so we must have seemed to the Scrawlings who came in, rowing Donar home themselves. They unloaded ivory, mostly, great bags of it on the jetty. But when Donar came up from the ship two men walked behind him, and another two behind them, and each pair carried between them what no one there but me had ever seen before, and that was an Elephant Tusk. And what tusks! You have never seen tusks like them, and never will, not out of Africa. Huge they were, and curled, and yellow with age, and each stood two men high.

So Donar came in state, marching to the gate of Asgard. He stopped before us Asers, grouped before Valhall, and the two pairs of bearers brought up one tusk on either side of him, upright, reaching far above our heads. Donar stuck his chest out and said,

'Here are the teeth of the World Serpent. No more will he wander the dark and bring down the hillsides, for I have killed him. With my little hammer I did it, all alone with my little Mollnir,' and he waved the hammer around his head, and I would not have called it a little hammer, though it was not of the largest, but there, I am no craftsman. The Asers all cheered, and the Scrawlings all screamed, and the Vandals shouted their warcries and banged their spear-butts on their shields. That night in Valhall, Donar stood up and told us all about it.

'Here I stand,' he began, 'too drunk to fall.'

'You're not,' shouted a number of the drunker Vandals but indeed he was, for he hadn't stopped drinking since I gave him his first horn, no not a cup, a horn, of Honeydew in the courtyard that morning.

'Here I stand,' he started again, 'as soused as a herring. I am only a poor smith, I can only hammer, I can't make up songs like some I could touch with a short stick, only hammer, hammer, hammer with the little Mollnir.' He was waving the hammer about, and suddenly flung it straight down the Hall. It just missed the minstrel, who flung himself flat in time, but scattered a brazier. And so he got first singed, and then wet, for someone threw over him one of the buckets that we kept standing round in case of fire, full of marsh water to start with, but of course they usually got topped up by anyone who had a skinful of beer and couldn't make it to the open air. But Bragi put out his hand and plucked the hammer out of the air, gently, and sent it back hard and fast to Donar, who went on:

'Here I stand, a poor smith who had some luck in the north. I'm not going to make a song about it, I can't, I can see two whetstones, two boars, four of those horrible birds. We didn't have any birds in the ship, just me and the Scrawlings, and we rowed the old barge north till we came to the edge of the ice. My hands were horny, my bottom was blistered, I'd had enough of rowing I'll tell you that. We left it there, and we got off and walked in the snow, and on our feet we wore great big boats for shoes.

'Far in the north we came to the hall of the Scrawling King. He had not built it of timber and turves and plaster, but of birchen boughs and deer skin over all. There we stopped to feast and to drink all through the winter and all through the night. There were Scrawling matrons to pour us our beer, and Scrawling maidens to help us to bed, and Scrawling magicians who did us great wonders such as we never see in Valhall the Great.'

At this he threw me Mollnir, and with rolled up sleeves I tossed the hammer up into the rafters and it didn't come down again. Instead, at intervals I plucked out of the air and passed to Donar a rose, a silk handkerchief, a couple of live pigeons, some horse-dung on a leaf which he passed to the minstrel, a gold cup of Honeydew, and an egg. When he had drunk the Honeydew he broke the egg into the cup, stirred it round with the point of his knife, and poured it over Baldur's head. And all that with never a pause in his flow of speech.

'Now the way that the sun goes round and round brings a snag you may not have noticed. Where the night is half a year long, there is only one night in the year. You eat when you're hungry, go to bed when you're . . . sleepy, and snore when you're dead beat. And better it is to sleep than to wake when the Earth Serpent walks. Aye, better it is to die without waking, to sleep and not see the Earth Serpent approaching, with great teeth for tearing and crunching the breast bone. His breath strikes cold, it is rank, and it stinks of the holes and the caves at the roots of the earth. There dwell the Scrawlings he kills in the Northlands, for any man who goes out in the snow, who goes out in the dark, to wander alone, the Earth Serpent takes him, to be, to exist, not to die, not to live, in anguish and misery down in his burrow under the roots of the earth.'

To rub in this point I passed Donar a human skull, which he stood fondling till it turned of a sudden into a sheep's stomach, stuffed and boiled, a dish of which the Germans are extremely fond, and then he threw it to the minstrel who ate it all, even the casing.

'When morning was near, or spring, whichever you like, and once in a while for a space the sky would lighten and show us a morsel of twilight in the gloom, I heard once at dinner, as we often did, the howling and skirling and scream as the Serpent went by. I was full as an egg, I was oiled as an owl, I was drunk as a Lord, as a King, as an Aser, I said to the King, to old Jokuhai-inen, I'll go out today and I'll kill the Earth Serpent!

'I put on my boats and I went out in the snow, and all I took with me was my hammer, my own little Mollnir, my dear little Mollnir.'

I let him have it back, and it dropped from the rafters on to the table with a crash and he picked it up and brandished it in the most dangerous manner all the rest of the evening.

'They were all drunk or they'd never have let me go, and old Jokuhai-inen, well he was the drunkest of all. But of course, if you've got to stay and stew up there, in darkness from summer's end to summer's beginning, what else is

126

there to do but drink to drown your dreams? So out I went, my hammer in my hand, my belly full of beer, to meet the Serpent and the terror that wanders in the winter woods.

'I walked through the pine wood, I walked through the fir wood, I walked through the scrub land of birches and alders, I met the hare, and I met the fox, I met the wolf and the lynx and the stoat, I met the creatures that walk in the winter, but nowhere could I find the Serpent tracks, though I could hear his voice shrill in the air, and feel the snow tremble beneath my boats. The dark was thick about me, it filled my lungs, my eyes, and my mouth and my hands, it flowed like water or tar, and all I could hear was the noise of the Serpent as he hunted me, as I hunted him.

'Then sudden without warning, the Serpent was on me. He kicked away the earth itself from beneath me, and pulled me down. I felt the huge snake body, cold as death, all round and thick and long. I felt his long smooth teeth, and I smelt his breath, all foul and stinking of death and cold as the dead. I shouted, to cheer myself, all the war cries I knew, and I struck with the hammer again and again and again. I heard the bone crack and splinter, and the beast let me go, and flung me down on the ground – and by then I was sober.

'I saw a light far off across the snow, and I thought another demon was come against me, so I took up Mollnir again and I walked towards it. But it was King Jokuhai-inen, sword in hand, come out to find my body in the snow. And none of all his warriors would come with him, except a small boy who came out to carry the torch. His name was Leminkai-inen, remember it, and he was the bravest Scrawling you ever will see. This summer I will make him a sword, and send it back when Jokuhai-inen comes in the Autumn.

'We went back to the Hall, and I got drunk again as soon as I could, to forget the horrible smell of the Serpent and death. When I die, my brothers, do not lay me in Earth, for the Serpent to suck out my eyes and lick clean my bones. Let me go to water or ice, or even to air, or best of all, as a smith, let me go to fire. But not to the earth, my friends, not to the earth . . .

127

·When Spring, or morning, had come, and every day had morning and eve, and something in between we could call day, we went out, the King and I, to find the Earth Serpent again. Where a river ran down through the winter wood, and the banks steeped down to the water, there the Serpent had burst from the earth and there the bones were lying. The wolves and the weasels and all the other vermin that feed on the carrion their betters have killed for them, had stripped away the flesh and gone off with full round bellies.

'Only the tail remained, long, round and thick, and at the end an anus split into two passages for all the world like nostrils. There too the skull, the forehead stove in and shattered, where Mollnir had struck and broken through to the brain box. Greatest of all were the teeth that lay before the skull, and those I brought home to show that my tale is true.'

Then the Scrawlings and the Vandals and everybody shouted and beat on the tables, and Donar once again shouted all the war cries he knew.

But I for one never believed there was an Earth Serpent, but I did not dare say so lest I be accused of slandering Donar. I remembered what I had heard among the Polyani, and I am sure that Donar came on one of the Mamunts as it broke from the earth, and that even as he came on it, it was dying or already dead. And he wounded it badly enough to kill again, and what he took for its tail, that was too tough to eat, was in fact its trunk.

The evening came to an uproarious end, and we played all the games and we muttonboned the minstrel, who left next day. Somehow we had difficulty in keeping our minstrels and we usually had to make do with Blind Hod, who wasn't much good as a minstrel. Come to that, he wasn't really blind either, but could see a little. Loki once sold him a bean-shaped piece of glass, which he swore was the emerald his late Sainted Majesty Nero had looked through, and indeed Hod found it very useful, but in the end Freda begged it from him to mount in silver and hang on a chain round her neck.

When the feasting was over, the Scrawlings took the silver for all the walrus ivory, and sailed back. But that silver was not wholly lost, for I sent a man to Sigmund, who caught them and their ship off Bornholm. He kept the ship and the silver, but the men he sold off south through Loki, who sent me my share. For we all three agreed that personal disagreements should not stand in the way of honest trade.

9

When I reached my own hall, Freda's time was come. I took care not to be too much around, but not too near either, and while Freda's birth screams filled Asgard I sat at the gate and haggled for pots of wine and bolts of linen. When Skirmir's wife came out to tell me I had a son, I went and brought him out to show the Asers, not in my arms, but cradled in my great Goth shield. And that is why we called him Scyld, which is the Goth word for a shield. We placed a sword in his hand, a tiny sax that Donar had made ready, and then we put wealth in his fingers, and we rubbed his fingers with wine and oil and honey, and we made his shield cradle soft with silk and furs. But the first thing he touched was a weapon.

After that I was less in Asgard than ever, because there is nothing I like less than a crying baby at night, and I much preferred to sit up at feasts and earn my headaches that way, if I *had* to get them.

About that time, Donar made me a helmet. He remembered the great parade helmets he had seen south of the Danube – Aristarchos had a splendid one – and he made me the nearest he could to that. It was a cap of iron with a ridge from nose to nape. The neck piece came down to protect my spine, and side guard for my cheeks. It left plenty of room inside to pile my hair for padding, as was the custom. You could always tell a Vandal by his topknot in those days.

Then he made me a face piece, with a nose and moustaches. The eyebrows he worked with boars set with garnets, and the ends of the eyebrows were the boar's head. Bragi carved shallow on wood the scenes of my own real life, Apollo and Artemis, the death of Grude and the treaty with the kings, and he beat out plates of bronze, thin as vellum and moulded them over the carved wood, and fitted them to the helmet, and gilded them.

This he did in the smithy next to the black shed where a hundred now watched the Honeydew. Snake swords we sold, the swords that would cut two bodies at one stroke. Honeydew we never sold. We gave it away.

Yes, we gave it away, free. The Germans would give their eyes for a smell of the stuff, so we let them have it free, as a gift, after a sale had gone through. In hope of a cup, a sip of Honeydew, a man would cut short his bargaining, bring down his price, forget to weigh his silver, measure the cloth, look for moth holes in the furs. We gave the liquor away, it was more profitable. But no Aser ever gave something for nothing.

Pictland

1

It was boring in Asgard that Spring. Freda was pregnant again, and I never got a chance to play with Scyld, Donar always had him. So when Cutha Cuthson came by and said I ought to go with him to the Saxons for some sea fishing, I went.

'It's not only the sea fishing,' he told me one evening on the way. 'It's my daughter.'

'The Queen?'

'The Queen. Mad on horses she is, and she leads the women in the dance, like her mother did after the old queen, Edwin's first wife, died. She wants Sleipnir for her mares, wants to improve the blood.'

I learnt more about the Saxons as we went on.

'Edwin's had bad luck. First of all there was his wife died giving birth to Harold, and he didn't take another. Well that's all right, there was always, let us say, the possibility of fertility that only a fertile king can give to a nation. But then Harold was going north to marry Gambara, and the Black Danes caught him in the Strait.

'Then we were able to persuade Edwin to get married again, and he married Edith, reasonable, I'm the richest Saxon there is, not to speak of being Edwin's cousin. But that was three years ago, and there's no sign of any heir. Some people are beginning to grumble. In the old days, of course, there would have been no hesitation, he'd have been ploughed in to make the barley grow the first barren spring, but now – well, we know there's a lot more to being a king

131

besides the barley. There's the herring shoals to foretell, and the whales to call to shore, and treaties to make with the Friesians and the price of salt to fix . . . and besides, Edith won't have it, and if she won't have it the women won't have it.'

The first few days at Edwin's hall on the edge of the salt beaches were taken up in games. Or at least in one game, the Head Game. There were two villages involved. They took a Batavian that had been shipwrecked, and that they had kept in a cage for the purpose, and someone cut off his head. The King threw the head up in the air, and the two villages fought for it. There were no weapons used, not even sticks, but three men died, two who burst when they were running, and one who got sat on by a couple of hundred men when he had the head in his hands. I had a busy week after that looking at sprains and bruises. The village that took the head within their own gates kept it and put it up on a stake and were proud of it.

This game lasted for three days. The two villages were unequally matched, which was why it took so short a time to finish.

Each night in hall we talked, and Edith sat with us at high table. I must say she was very taken up with her horses. She had grown up with horses – Cutha was the chief horse master of the Saxons – and she kept on bringing the conversation back to them, till at last I said to her,

'You shall have Sleipnir for your mares, tomorrow.'

It was two days later that we went, riding alone, the two of us, with a gelding led behind for my return. The mares were, of course, in the Grove where they worship the Mother.

When we came to the fence of living thorns that surround the Grove, we dismounted. I wondered already that she should take a stallion into such a place. We unsaddled Sleipnir outside, and turned him loose to run with the mares. Then to my surprise and horror Edith took my arm and led me toward the gate in the fence. I stood still.

'Come!' she cried. 'What are you afraid of? Little bears? I tell you, there is no woman here but me.'

'Except the Mother.'

'The Mother? I suppose you think there is no Mother, or that I am the Mother? I tell you, Votan, the Mother sleeps, and she shall sleep here till a man wakes her – a man, Votan, not a god, or a half-god, or an Aser.'

'The guilt is on you,' I told her, 'for you, that profane this place, are a queen.'

'A queen?' She looked at Sleipnir galloping toward the white mares. 'What is a queen? I am not a queen. I am only Cutha Cuthson's daughter. I've never been anything else. Married to Edwin I may be, but a queen, never.'

'But if you are the king's wife, then you are queen.'

'What is a king, then? A king is the luck of his people. It is the king who calls the fish to the shallows, or the ships to wreck. The king is the luck of his people. It is the king who charms away scabs and brings rain and makes the corn to grow. A fertile king makes fertile all the nation. And if he is not fertile?'

Ploughed in to make the grass grow, I thought. She read my mind.

'Would you have that happen to Edwin? Would you have it happen to the Saxons? Without him the whole nation would split up, some to be Danes and some Friesians and some Lombards. Or worse, dissolve into a thousand leaderless families like the Vandals, and serve foreigners for a crust of bread.'

We watched Sleipnir among the mares. She spoke again, bitterly. She was nineteen; she was Cutha Cuthson's daughter. She had grown up in a mist of riches. No bog woman, she had heard all the tales of the merchants, all the gossip of the trade roads, all the songs of the bards. She had led the women in the dance before the Mother, as her mother had done when there was no queen. She was bitter.

'What then, is a queen? She is the living proof of the king's luck. Her fertility shows forth his power. How can he crop the fields if he cannot crop her?'

She took my elbow. She sensed my reluctance, my fear. 'What's the matter, Votan? Do you think we will cut you

133

in pieces, you who hung on the tree? Last night I burnt the blade bone and I watched the fat on the pot, and I know you will see lands the Riders never knew. I saw your life, Votan, and it will be long.'

We came to the cart, the Mother's cart. It was high built on man-high wheels of foot-thick elm. The frame was of ash, and the panels of lime, carved and painted with the rites of the Mother. The roof was pointed, and thatched with barley straw. There was a door in the end and steps to it.

Outside the thorn fence I had left my spear and my knife, the only iron things I had. Here before the cart I laid aside my bronze cloak fastener and my gold armlet. The foot of the steps must serve for the threshold, and there I did what else was necessary. Edith had chosen as wisely as she knew, a stranger, a wandering man without father and without a nation, yet a man of wealth and power, known to be potent his wife with child again. Now by what I did at the steps she knew that I was no stranger to the Mother.

We paid our duties to the Mother. She was here carved roughly, no not even carved, chopped with an adze out of the ash whose shape She still kept. Before Her was Her bed down mattress and down quilt, covered with sheets of linen

Later I asked Edith,

'Why a cart? Why, here, a cart?'

'Votan! That *you* should ask.' She laughed. All the tenseness and bitterness was gone. She stood naked and went to the door, and took from hands unseen cups, and a jug of barley beer, and barley bread, still warm, and deer meat smoking hot.

'Long, long ago, the Women tilled the earth and worshipped the Mother. The horse gave us no more than the cow meat and hide and hair. Then the Mother lived, as we did in houses, or caves, and, in the heat, in groves and woods

'The Riders came out of the east. They worshipped only the cruel sky that sends snow and sun to torment us. They swung their great iron swords from their high, high horses and they took the poor Mother from her groves, and shut her in a cart to travel the roads of the world for ever.'

134

'So now it is the Mother, and not the king who makes the corn to grow?'

She giggled.

'So they say, so they say. What do the men know of what we do or whom we honour? Yet, the days of the kings who are kings because they make the crops are ending. Soon they will give way to kings who are kings because they are born of the Gods themselves.

'I tell you, Votan, from this day on, there is no man in all the Saxon tribes who will move to bring down Edwin. No woman will let her man depose Edith's husband. Yet the men will never know why the women are so much against civil war, when there have been other times . . . Votan, you came when the Mother called.'

Late in the afternoon we went down the steps. I put on my bronze buckled shoes and someone had waxed them. I picked up my bronze fastened cloak, and someone had wiped the mud from it, and ironed it. I left the gold armband where it lay. We walked to the gap in the hedge, and I saw it was a hedge of thorned roses and the buds that had been when we entered were now full flowers.

2

Eventually, I got my day of sea fishing. I went down to the jetty in the grey and chilly dawn and looked at the boat. It was quite big, about twenty paces long, clinker built, with overlapping planks, not nailed or dowelled together, but sewn, rib to keel and plank to rib with juniper withies. She was undecked and there was a rickety tabernacle for a mast, but no mast or sail in the boat. I asked Edward, the owner, if he were going to take them. He looked at the grey sky and spat.

'Good fishing day, and it'll be dead calm. No use taking mast or sail. You know the great rules up here for foretelling the weather?'

'No,' I said. 'Not up here.'

'Well, the first is this. The best forecast for tomorrow's weather is a description of today's, whatever that may be. The second is this: any change will be for the worse for your purpose, whatever that may be. Stands to reason, any change will mean an offshore wind, to make us row back against it, and what use will a sail be then? Unless, that is, you have any other ideas.'

It is sometimes embarrassing to be a manifestation, however imperfect, of a weather god. I declined to interfere, and we got in.

This was the only time I went anywhere without Gungnir. I left it leaning behind Edwin's high table. I had good clothes on, too, good to go fishing in Edith had said, with a gold chain and a couple of rings and a big morse of gold and garnets to fasten my grey cloak. I had no sword of any kind, only my knife.

There were twelve Saxons in the boat when we pushed off. There was the usual jumble of gear and fishing lines in the bottom of the boat, looking in complete confusion the way it always does at sea, till the time comes to do anything, and then you find how carefully it was all stowed. Ten men rowed, with light chopping strokes. The oldest man, Ethelbert, leaned over the bow and took us out over the shallows and the sandbanks to where we could expect fish.

I sat in the stern with Edward, who had the steering oar, of course, and we talked about the sea. After a while he grasped that I had handled ships before, though quite different ships in another sea, and he let me handle her for a bit. You couldn't tell in that flat calm, but the whole boat felt too limber by half. All the time I was in her, I was expecting those withies to wear through, all together, all at once, and leave us floundering in the water.

Now just when Ethelred had picked up the anchor, which was a courtesy term for a big stone with a rope tied to it, the wind came. It was just as when you tilt the jug and the liquid comes rushing out of it all at once. One moment there was no wind at all, just a flat calm; the next moment it was blowing from hard astern, just a little off the sirocco, south

136

of south-east. It was howling and blowing and we were going up and down enormous waves. I had never seen or heard anything like it, and neither had the Saxons. Edward and I laid on the steering oar.

'What about getting her head round?' I shouted. 'Aren't you afraid of being pooped?'

'No,' he bawled back. 'Pooped we may be this way, but if I come round, we'll be swamped for sure broadside on.'

'Your boat,' I told him. 'You know how she handles,' and I hoped he did.

He was right. We found we could hold her fairly steady with two men on the steering oar. Ethelred came aft, and tied a line on a bucket and threw it overboard. We all gasped as we saw the way the line whisked out, and we never did get the bucket back. It was a good bucket, too.

After an hour we were out of sight of land. The sky was still overcast, not raining, but grey, and there was still that wind. A little later we could see a blue smudge to port. Edward waved his arms at it.

'That's the Holy Island. Nobody lives there. Past that and we're in the great sea.'

Nobody ever likes to be out of sight of land, certainly not on a strange sea. There were all kinds of tales about this sea, how it was solid with fish and so on, and by logic if you went across it you should reach Britain. But who wanted to go to Britain that way when all you needed to do was to go down the coast to Boulogne, slip across and then coast north or west to wherever you wanted to go?

But drifting out to sea had happened to other people before, always to other people. If it happened to you once and you ever came back, it usually put you off going to sea again. Therefore Edward had been careful to bring drinking water and a little food, sun-dried beef and twice-baked bread. The water casks were full; I had seen that done before we went aboard.

A little way outside the Holy Island we saw something horrible. We came to the crest of a wave and we saw another ship. She was about half a mile away. She had a sail set,

137

and drawing, and she was making reasonable way, not fast, but enough, and right before the wind – her wind. For while our wind drove us west of north, she was making north of east. We went across her bows, our tracks at right angles.

Out of Richborough for the Saxon coast, the Saxons agreed, and they argued among themselves about her cargo, and all this to drown the thought that this was our own private wind, blowing for us alone. Only one man came aft, called Osbert, and he asked,

'Has any of you wronged a Scrawling?'

'No,' said Edward, and Osbert went on,

'Because the yellow Scrawlings in the east, they keep the winds in a bag, and when any one wrongs them they let out for him an evil wind.'

'And then?'

'He gets blown out to sea, and over the edge of the world. And that's the end.'

'Don't be stupid,' I said, in as superior a tone as I could manage. 'Why do you think I came fishing today?'

I leant back in the stern and looked as confident as I could and occasionally said things like,

'Hold her steady there,' or,

'That's fine, dead on course.'

I remembered how Jokuhai-inen could bring the winds to his whistle and I remembered the Scrawlings that brought back Donar and that Loki had sold for me. I knew that if I let the Saxons think that this wind was sent against me I would be overboard in no time. I dare not, therefore, ask if they had any salt or garlic on board. If I had brought Gungnir I might have tried to cut the wind, I remembered the proper things to say, but I didn't want to try with only a knife. So I sat back and let them think, without my saying so, that the wind wasn't sent against us, but that I had brought it.

Toward evening, Edward issued a ration of water, not much. I had my old waterbottle, on its strap, full of hydromel, and we didn't dare let the men know about that, so Edward and I hid it under the nets and sat on it. Albert, who was a careful dresser, came aft and went on the oar.

For the night we tied ourselves to the thwarts, for the boat was rolling and pitching together in a most unpleasant spiral motion. Some of the Saxons were sick. At dawn we had water and dried meat, and at noon we had water and some fish we had caught, raw. During the nights we were kept awake all the time by men clambering over us to relieve the steersmen and to hold us end on, any end on, to the howling wind that blew out of nowhere. Yet no one suggested offering a sacrifice of what we had to Wude.

Toward noon on the third day we saw land, quite close, for the boat was very low in the water. It was a low green shore, with two or three strange green hills like upturned buckets, and an island a little offshore of the same shape. There was more land visible to starboard. We were in the mouth of a river. Suddenly the wind dropped, stopped, just like that. The Saxons left off arguing whether we were off Britain or Ireland or the Land of Norroway, and with one accord began to row for the nearer shore. I said nothing; I was sure our troubles weren't over.

When we were close in, the current changed, the tide began to tug at the boat, and we were carried out to sea again, the oarsmen crying and cursing as they heaved. It was no use. Out we went, north and east, out of sight of land. We spent another night at sea, still under that black blanket of cloud, with nothing to tell us even which way we were going.

By now the lashings that held the boat together were in a bad way. Edward and Ethelred had spent most of the voyage crawling about in the bottom finding frayed withies and replacing them from a supply that they carried, but now there were no more fresh withies left. We had had two men baling all the way, but now we had four. We were no longer rationed on water; we were more likely to drown than to die of thirst.

3

Now and then through the night we thought we heard waves
on the beach. Once Albert said he saw a light, and we tried
to believe him. When dawn came, we found we were in an
estuary, but either further in or in a different one. Now we
had flat land with sand dunes on either side. The clouds
had changed into a thin haze through which we could see
the rising sun.

It was the tide that was carrying us in, said the Saxons,
though what these tides are or how they are produced I could
never understand. They do not happen according to any
regular rule of time. Anyway, this tide carried us in over
the shoals and glad we were to be in water that at least we
would be able to wade through, for at the first oar stroke
the boat creaked and let in water at a dozen places.

We were now sitting up to our waists in water, and yet
we were reluctant to get out of the boat while it would still
carry us. When at last it grounded we got over the side and
we were no wetter than we had been. We couldn't get the
boat afloat again, for the tide had left her stranded on a
sandbank. Once the support of the water was taken away
she began to break up under her own weight. The wonder
was that she had held together so long. I noticed that it was
only now that she was dying that I began to think of the
boat as she and not as it.

We took what was worth salvaging, knives and saxes and
what food we had and my flask of hydromel. We had a long
walk ashore, from ankle deep water to slushy mud, but it
would have been much farther had we not come in at the
highest point of the tide. When we reached the line of
seaweed and wood chippings and rubbish on the high tide
mark we looked back. Our boat was already in ruins. Farther
out on the water there were half a dozen other boats, big
ones, full of men. We could see the glint of metal.

In front of us, about half a mile away or less, there was

a village, a cluster of huts. We could hear all the land noises we had not heard for days, dogs barking, children quarrelling, and the wonderful noise of women grinding corn. We could hear them at that distance, and that was a wonder seeing what lay in between. There stood a long line of spearmen, about a hundred of them, and on their flank, on our right flank, at right angles to their shield wall there was a long line of bowmen strung out to enfilade our charge on the shieldless side.

The weapons were the ones we were used to, spear, long sword, shield. The man who walked forward in front of his soldiers to address us was clad in familiar clothes, trousers, tunic, cloak, but his cloak came down almost to his heels, not to the hips like the German cloak. All his clothes were worked in an intricate pattern of red and yellow lines on a green ground. That much was strange, but his face was stranger still. As he came forward his face looked dark. At his nearest we saw it was blue!

A few yards from us he stopped and drew his sword while his little army stood stock still and waited, the spears at the ready and arrow feathers back to the shoulder. He placed the weapon carefully on the ground and drew back. The meaning was clear.

'Do it!' I said.

'May as well now as later,' grumbled Edward. He unbuckled his sword belt and laid it on the sand. We all followed suit. I laid down my knife. Then we stepped back a few paces. There seemed a general agreement among the Saxons to leave me nearest to the arrows.

Another man came forward and picked up all the swords and tucked them under his arm. Blue Face seemed to be keeping a tally, notching a piece of wood. They took the swords only, they even left the sheaths, some of them beautifully ornamented, and they left our knives, the kind of things you use for cutting your meat and trimming your toenails.

Blue Face came further forward. He spoke to us. He spoke at length with considerable eloquence. With fine gestures

141

of his sensitive fingers, with exquisite modulations of tone, he went through a complex reasoned argument. It took some time. It was a pity none of us understood a word.

When he had finished I stepped forward. I told him in German that we were simple fishermen, shipwrecked by no fault of our own, and that we were men of substance at home, and I for one had enough gold on me to buy another boat.

He explained, unintelligibly, but perfectly clearly, that I was just as unintelligible to him. I tried in Greek, but this got no response. Then I spoke in Latin, and he brightened up. At least he recognised the language, even if he couldn't understand it.

He pointed inland and said,

'Rex, Rex. Venite. Tutti, venite.'

This I took to mean that he was going to take us to his King, and that we would be safe . . . safe there, or safe till we got there? I didn't even bother to tell the Saxons, I just left them to trust me.

Then Blueface pointed to himself and said,

'Morien.'

I took this to be his name, and I answered in the same way.

'Votan.'

Morien thumped his own chest again and, as I found later, recited his pedigree which began 'Morien map Seissyllt map Kynedr Wyllt map Hettwn Glavyrawc map Llwch.' I only caught the first word, so when he finished I said again 'Votan'.

Morien Blueface, who all this time had not approached nearer than twenty paces, motioned us to sit down on the dry sand, which we did. Then he walked away, and so did his little army, back to the village. Only about thirty spearmen, young men, came and formed a circle around us. These men, all wearing cloaks of the same red and yellow and green pattern as Morien sat down, each man with his spear across his knees. Some of them had dogs, great ugly things, fit to tackle a wolf alone, two to settle a bear.

After an hour or so, some children came out with food for the guards. After a lot of giggling and encouragement

142

from their big brothers, they brought some into the circle for us. There was beer, good beer, and plenty of boiled bacon, and big flat cakes of bread, hot, baked on stones, and not of wheat, but of some other corn, millet I thought.

It got warmer, and some of the Saxons went to sleep, and some of the spearmen looked as if they wanted to. One or two of the other Saxons were talking loudly about not being ordered about and one Saxon being worth ten Scrawlings. I spoke to them pretty sharply.

'Once outside this circle and I will no longer protect you. Stay here and do what I tell you, and you will be safe.'

That seemed to calm most of them down, but of course it had to be Albert who would keep on walking about and going up to the spearmen in an experimental way. None of them so much as looked at him. Then, all of a sudden he was out of the circle and running like a hare for the edge of the woods. The spearmen didn't follow him, they all came up to their feet and to the ready. The dogs moved, though, and before he had gone a hundred yards they had him down. A crowd came running out of the village, and we could hear Albert yelling. A man came out of the crowd carrying Albert's clothes. We realised that the rest of the crowd were all women. Suddenly the yelling stopped, and all the women came away. There was no sign of Albert. We remembered it was the first of May.

Our guards seemed as frightened as we were. The Saxons realised that these men were there to protect us, not to restrain us. The man came up and placed Albert's clothes in front of me. He seemed very concerned about the way the dog had torn the trousers. The belt and knife were there, and two rings and a neck chain, and Albert's ear-rings that he always wore, with blood on them. We all sat down again. We didn't talk about it.

After another three hours or so, Morien came down from the village. He made a face as he passed the stain on the sand where we had last seen Albert. We all wondered what happened next. I remembered the shipwrecked sailors we had thrown into the bog.

When Morien came close to us, we saw that his face was not really blue. It was tattooed in a close and intricate pattern of blue lines so that little pink skin showed. On each cheek was a crescent moon, on its back, with a line that went up to each corner of his eyes. On each jaw bone, around each temple, writhed a snake with a horse's head. Eels wriggled up his arms, five headed eels, a head on each fingertip.

He took me by the arm.

'Rex, Rex,' he said. 'Ad Rex Venite.'

I went with him toward the water's edge. The Saxons and the spearmen followed. I wondered if we were going to ford the river, which looked a mile wide, when I saw men running down from the village carrying boats, big boats, two men to a boat as if they weighed nothing.

When we came to the water's edge and got in we found they did weigh nothing to speak of, They were made of a wicker frame covered with leather. Seal, I found, is the best leather for the purpose, which is why we hardly ever got any seal fur through Asgard. The boats were short and round, with two thwarts. This meant two Saxons and four spearmen in each boat, except that Edward and I each had five Saxons to look after us. Morien came in my boat. He tried to keep as far to windward of me as he could; I suppose he found the smell of my pig fat strange.

It was now clear that we had been waiting for the tide to turn. Villagers held bobbing boats for us to get in. They ballasted them with stones. Old millstones are the best, with no sharp corners. If a Briton tells you he sailed the seas on a millstone, that is what he means.

Yes, a Briton. I was already quite clear about that. Tattooed men, great brindled dogs, patterns like the Gauls wear, where else could we be? The only question was whether we were inside or outside the Empire, going to a British puppet king or a real Pictish one?

With the tide and the paddles, for the rowers faced forward and scooped the boats along, we went up stream as fast as a man might walk and much more comfortably. We kept it up for hours, and at sunset we pulled in to a village. We

144

had to; we were well out of the influence of the tide, and the stream was getting too shallow.

The headman came down to the shore and greeted Morien with great deference. A crowd of people and animals were turned out of a house to make way for us, and all the Saxons were ushered in. It was a big house. The spearmen turned paddlers turned back into spearmen again, and slept outside. If I am any judge, Morien had the headman's hut, and his supper and his wife into the bargain.

We got the same supper as our guards, and like them nobody's wife, though after what had happened to Albert we had no wish to meet any more British women. They gave us porridge, like the stuff the legionaries eat, but not wheat. It was a grain called oats, and they grow it in the Land of Norroway too, where the weather is always too wet for real corn to ripen.

The spearmen put salt on their porridge and ate it like that, but the Germans found it unpalatable. The spearmen laughed and brought pitchers of honey and warm milk which we mixed with it, and then the stuff was edible.

We curled up to sleep on the floor, wrapped up in our cloaks and what blankets had been left. There was more left than blankets, and we were soon scratching; new fleas came to avenge their comrades drowned at sea.

At dawn we were awakened with platters of bacon and a black greasy substance fried up with oatmeal. I wondered what it was, being so tasty, and in the end it turned out to be the boiled seaweed I had always refused to look at, let alone eat, at home in Valhall.

We got outside the house and mingled with our escort. The huts were round. German huts are square, or oblong, foursided anyway. In Britain the smaller houses are round. These particular houses looked flimsy and ramshackle as if they were only intended to last for a few weeks, and that was just the case. It was what they called a Havod, a summer place, where the young lads and girls lived looking after the cattle through the summer. The young men, the nobles of course I mean, go to spend three years at the king's court in his warband. There they learn to make war, and they ride the forest and guard the havods, and catch cattle thieves from other tribes, or perhaps steal a few cattle themselves. There is small difference between keeping and taking.

It was of course a party of these young men, from the king's family as they say, who had been ready to catch us on the shore, and now, under Morien the head of that village, were taking us to their King.

After breakfast, we were mounted on shaggy little ponies, smaller than the German horses. The Saxons kept on falling off; they are the worst horsemen I have ever seen, and proud of it. But we moved away from the river along a great ride cut through the wood, for cattle droving I suppose.

After a long day's ride, with a stop at another havod for a meal of oat cakes and cheese and cold bacon and warm milk, we came in sight of a city. Yes, a city! Not a city like Rome or Athens, but a city that Homer or Hesiod would have recognised. There were a hundred or so houses gathered around a market place, and above it on the hilltop were the walls of an Acropolis.

We reached the market place and stopped, and we took another step back to Homer. There was a blowing of horns, and Morien waved to us to dismount, and some of the Saxons slid off, and others fell off. Then we saw something that only lived for us in legends. We saw chariots!

These were not racing chariots like the ones you see at the games, those are only coachbuilders' fancy. These were real war chariots. I saw plenty in later years, but these were my first. They had wicker bodies, and bronze fittings, and six-foot wheels to go bounding over rough ground. Each had two horses harnessed to the pole. That, of course, is the trouble. You know you can never get cavalry to charge twice in one day; even if you can get them all back together again, they're blown. You're lucky if you can get chariots to charge once, certainly not if you have to cover more than two hundred yards. It chokes the horses. There's absolutely no future in trying to use horses to pull vehicles, unless you can find some way of not tying the harness around their necks, and if nobody's thought of a way by now they never will.

Each of these was a three-man chariot. The first and the last were purely military, even if they had unshipped the long knives they fasten on the sides to discourage anyone getting too close. They each carried a very small driver, and two other men, bowmen, again very small.

The second was more ornate. The driver was very small. The other passengers were both quite big men, one old, one fairly young. Each of them was dressed in loose white clothes. They were clean-shaven and short-haired, both red-headed. Each wore on his head a garland of oak leaves. Each had on his breast a fresh sprig of mistletoe. These then were the priests of Britain I had heard of, the Druids, the Pythagoreans.

The third chariot, though, was the important one. The driver was a big middle-aged man, in patterned clothes, the same pattern as Morien. There were gold bracelets, gold chains, gold armbands enough to show that he was rich. The great gold collar above his neck and breast showed that he was royal, the gold diadem in his hair showed that he was a king. The brindled hounds that followed the chariot wore collars of gold. Spearmen pressed about him. If ever there were a king in Britain, this was a great king, and a Pictish king at that.

And with him there was a woman. She was small of build, neat and trim in all her movements. Her hair was black, yet not the same black as our Greek girls. Her eyes were a light, innocent cornflower blue. But what her skin was like or how old she was, how could I tell? Her face, like the king's, like Morien's, like everyone else's in the whole company, except the two Druids, was covered in blue tattooing. A procession of crabs went clockwise round her forehead. An oystershell was on each cheek, and on each finger a sea horse's head was joined into one neck that ran up her arm beneath her sleeve.

The king, and the lady, stopped and looked at us. I thanked heaven that I was wearing a good suit of clothes, even if it had been four days at sea, and some gold. I stepped forward ready to act as spokesman for the whole crew, but the woman pointed at me, said a few words I couldn't understand, and they moved on. Still, I thought, it was something to catch the eye of royalty. I don't know how I'd have felt if I'd known then that what she said was,

'The one with the white hair, he looks tasty. I'll have him.'

4

There was then a good deal of confusion in the market place, as is usual after the great have gone by. Somehow I got separated from the Saxons, but the noises I heard later that night showed that nothing very dreadful had happened to them. Morien took my arm, and a few spearmen jostled me from behind, and before I knew it I was inside a house, and that is more difficult than it may sound. For these houses were like none in Germany; they were of stone. They were round, and walls of unhewn stone fitted together without mortar rose to shoulder height, and a pointed roof of poles and thatch rose twice as high again. There was a hole at the peak, to let the smoke out and the light in. There was a fire of peat, and even in May we needed it in the evenings.

The spearmen crowded in too. There was a stone bench around the walls, and they sat on that. They kept on changing over, but there were always enough there to make sure I stayed.

After a while Morien came in and they brought me food, porridge and bacon and baked meat and cheeses. I ate sucking pig, and lamb, and veal. I ate kid, and so I pushed aside one of the cheeses, which, by the smell, was goat. I left bear and goose. I ate duck. There was a dish of vegetables. I fished about in it with care, and I laid out eight beans on a plate, for the bean is sacred to the Pythagoreans and it would have been imprudent, at the least, to have eaten it with meat. Then I had another thought, and I went back to the dish, and I found another bean, and I laid them out on the plate in a square, three beans long and three beans

148

wide and three beans from corner to corner, three and three and three, the perfect number in the perfect form. Morien watched every move, and I hoped that he knew no more of the Pythagoreans than I. But at least he learned that I knew something.

When Morien and the empty dishes, for there was not much difference between them in attractiveness, went away, and we were left with a big pot of beer, I began to get bored drinking with people I couldn't talk to. So I wandered about the room, and after a little I was sitting looking at three cups and a nut, and the spearmen were looking at me. I remembered having an argument with a man in Alexandria as to whether you can do this if you haven't a chance to say anything. I found it possible, but rather difficult; it even helps to talk away earnestly in a language your audience don't understand.

I did quite well at first. I got a new pair of shoes, for mine were ruined with the salt water, and some leg wrappings, and a bone comb, and a mirror, and an embroidered belt, and an armband, silver set with polished pebbles. Then we all lay down to sleep round the fire, though some of the lads stayed awake all night arguing over how it was done.

They woke me at dawn with lots of food, porridge and bacon and seaweed. Never confess to a liking for anything in a foreign country; they try to ensure you live on nothing else. After a little while for digestion I turned my attention to a young man who hadn't been at the session the night before and wanted to know what we had been playing. I showed him, and won his cloak fastening; I didn't want it really, except on principle, but he *would* wager it against mine, and I suppose he thought he was cleverer than the rest. Suddenly the laughter of the game stopped abruptly. Among the players there was the young Druid from the chariot. He reached out and touched the cups.

He was good. Quite quickly he won from me the cloak fastener, the armband, the belt, the comb and the mirror. With a pointed gesture he left me the shoes. I passed him the cups. With a little difficulty – I said he was good –

I won back the cloak fastener, the armband, the belt and the mirror. With a pointed glance I left him the comb.

He combed his thick short red hair. He combed out of it a flea, a snail, a lizard, a mouse and a squirrel. They all sat on the table. I threw the end of my cloak over them, and they changed into a flock of pigeons which fluttered away through the chimney hole, leaving two eggs on the table. He stroked the comb, which turned into a centipede and wriggled off among the floor straw. I put the mirror on the coiled belt, and it turned into a frying pan full of sizzling fat over a crackling fire. I broke the two pigeons' eggs into the pan and had a second breakfast. I didn't offer the Druid any; I didn't think he deserved it.

None of this is very difficult if you know how, and so, having shown each other our professional credentials, we were free to talk. The Druid spoke first, in Latin, with a dreadful provincial accent and full of tricks of speech carried over from his own tongue.

'I am Taliesin. I am Himself, without Father, without Mother, born of the Oak, I live of the Oak. Photinus, Man without Kindred, are the Kindred that you are without the Kindred that I am without? Are you come of the tree I am come of? What then do you here? Man brought on the Wind, what did you there?'

'What does it matter to you what I have done, or what I will do?'

'Nothing, indeed, what you will do, for that is as much in our destinies as in yours, but it is out of interest and out of curiosity and out of inquisitiveness that I ask you what you did do, for you brought the Sun with you, and it is seldom enough that we see him, and three days running is unheard of. And it is known, and it is patent, and it is obvious, that the wind was your wind, for there was a singing in your praise all last night by your crew, and your shipmen, and your sailors.'

That I knew was an exaggeration, since the last thing I had heard Edward singing was a dreadful song called 'Knut, the Bastard King of Scania', and I will not trouble you with